ALEX KOHL

requiem
of
him

Of Solace & Sin Duet
Book 1

Copyright © 2025 by Alex Kohl

All rights reserved.

No part of this book may be reproduced in any form or by any electronic or mechanical means, including information storage and retrieval systems, without written permission from the author, except for the use of brief quotations in a book review. This is a work of fiction. Names, characters, places, and incidents are either products of the authors imagination or used in a fictitious manner. Any resemblance to actual persons, living or dead, or events is purely coincidental.

Cover design: designs_by.lm

Editing: Mat Mansfield

Formatting: Marie Ann

BLURB

Levi

Nearly a decade without him should be long enough to forget.

I've been watching him in secret for years.

He doesn't know who I am, and I planned to keep it that way.

The last thing I expected is for my carefully laid plans to go up in flames.

No one was ever supposed to find me.

We were never supposed to survive.

But how can I walk away when he's always been mine?

Cortland

Protecting someone from the shadows is always a risk.

Especially doing it for years and never laying eyes on them.

He ran and I didn't chase him.

He hid and I kept a careful distance knowing he was safe.

Safe from those who wanted nothing more than to see him in ruin.

What I didn't expect is for him to find me somewhere I should've never been.

But now that he's right in front of me, I can't fathom walking away a second time.

PLAYLIST

Theme Song: High Water — Sleep Token

I'd Rather See Your Star Explode — SLAVES
Skin and Bones — David Kushner
Someone Else — Loveless, Kellin Quinn
Shame On Me — Catch Your Breath
Wasted On You — Morgan Wallen
Heartless - Wallen Album Mix — Morgan Wallen
Mind On You — George Birge
Let This Haunt You — SLAVES
Bad Nature — Nerv
Judas — Banks
Different Man — Kane Brown, Blake Shelton
Closer — Nine Inch Nails
The Hand That Feeds — Nine Inch Nails
Ascensionism — Sleep Token
The Machine - Slowed — Reed Wonder, Aurora Olivas
Stained — KID BRUNSWICK
Every Day Is Exactly The Same — Nine Inch Nails
Make Believe — Memphis May Fire
Thinkin' Bout Me — Morgan Wallen
Novocaine — Too Close To Touch, Bad Omens
Watermelon Moonshine — Lainey Wilson

Wildflowers and Wild Horses — Lainey Wilson
Dial Tone — Catch Your Breath
Pretty Little Devil — Shaya Zamora
Fallout — Sleep Theory
Happier Than Ever — Billie Eilish
Still Don't Know My Name — Labrinth
Inbred — Ethel Cain
Crush — Ethel Cain
WILDFLOWER — Billie Eilish
Hurricane — Luke Combs
Take Me Back To Eden — Sleep Token
Come Hell or High Water — Imminence
The Offering — Sleep Token
Lies Lies Lies — Morgan Wallen
lovely liar — Stevie Howie
Another Way — Sleep Theory
Daddy's Mugshot — Laci Kaye Booth
Out Of Oklahoma — Lainey Wilson
Warm — SG Lewis
Rosemary — Deftones
Cities — Two Feet, Toby Mai
What It Cost — Bad Omens
Running Up That Hill — Placebo
Intoxicated — Warren Zeiders

For each of you who have been hurt by the hands meant to nurture and love, who have felt the sting of betrayal by those meant to protect you. But most of all, for each of you who are forced to remain in the shadows, shackled by circumstance rather than being given the freedom you deserve to live as you were meant to.

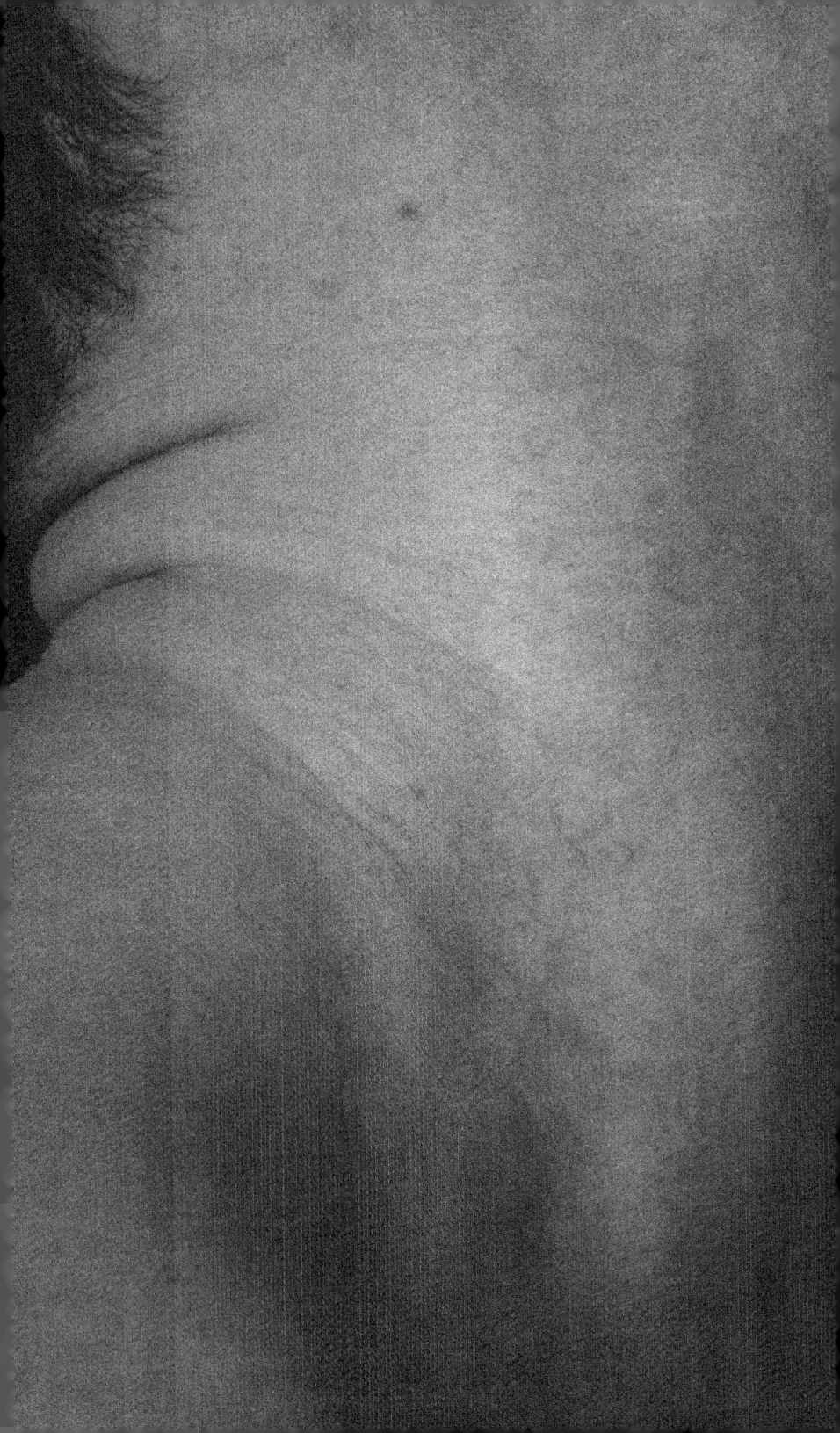

"I could recognize him by touch alone, by smell; I would know him blind, by the way his breaths came and his feet struck the earth. I would know him in death, at the end of the world."

—Madeline Miller 'The Song of Achilles'

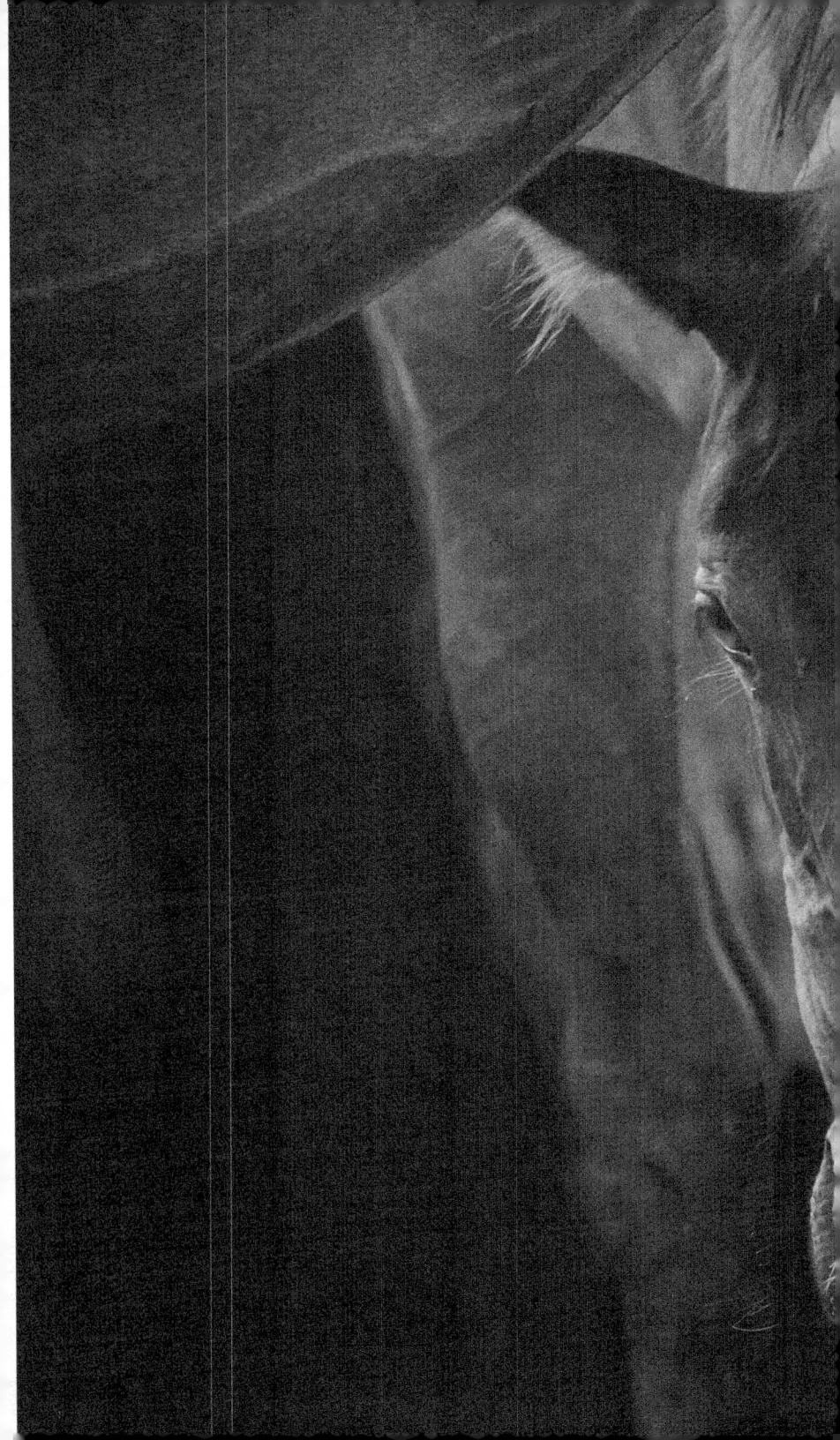

AUTHOR'S NOTE

As many of you may know, Requiem Of Him was not intended to be a debut release, but it happened that way for a reason I suppose. With that being said, I couldn't be happier because I love these boys more than I can even express.

Their story is not an easy one, but I knew that going into this with my eyes wide open. While they're messy and love to pick fights with one another, I couldn't have dreamed up a better pair. Levi is every bit, as my dear friend mentioned, like a kitten backed into a corner and absolutely ready to claw someone's eyes out without provocation. Cortland is the silent type of crazy and a snake in the grass, especially when he wants something…or someone.

Cortland and Levi are deeply flawed and at times the most frustrating characters to deal with—Cortland, I'm looking at you. I can confidently say they are unlike any character I've written before, especially Levi.

They are toxic, obsessive and downright nasty to each other, but that's just who they are. They aren't ever going to be the perfect, sickening sweet couple, and I love that about them. Even if I wanted them to get a grip, they wouldn't—they're a foregone conclusion at this point.

<u>Keep in mind that Requiem Of Him is book one of the Of Solace & Sin Duet and will end on a cliffhanger.</u> You will be left with a lot of questions and frustration at the end of this book, and rightfully so, but it is so worth it. They are worth it.

I guess that's all I've got for you. Enjoy and don't kill me when you finish it...I might like it ;)

CONTENT WARNING

The content of Requiem Of Him is a dark romance and may be triggering to some readers. Bear in mind that Requiem Of Him is book one of a duet and does end on a cliffhanger. <u>Below is a list of possible trigger warnings and specific content within the story, please be aware this list does contain spoilers.</u>

mention of suicide, mention of domestic violence, mention of child abuse, mention of aggressive animals, non-con/dubcon, rape, homophobia, transphobia, use of dead name, use of feminine anatomical terms, mention of drug use, mention of drug addiction, cheating, bodily fluids, watersports, spanking, slapping, overstimulation, humiliation, degradation, misgendering, anxiety/panic attacks, gender disphoria

PROLOGUE
EIGHT YEARS AGO

'Happier Than Ever' Billie Eilish

Branches whipped across my skin, stinging more each time they split the soft tissue of my cheeks as my feet beat against the mossy overgrown forest floor. Adrenaline spiked in my veins the further I managed to get from the hounds nipping at my heels, but one misstep would have me falling into their snapping jaws. The burning in my lungs was excruciating, but I couldn't stop—I had no choice but to make it to the other side.

I ran the moment I realized I was being watched for too long, too closely by those I should have been able to trust implicitly. I hadn't done anything. I wasn't guilty. I just wanted to live, to no longer feel the crushing weight of expectation and obligation. The punishment would never fit my alleged sins. I'd been painted by the same brush as my brothers and sisters who had come before me and the ones who would no doubt come after me.

An adulterer. A sycophant. An abomination. An inferior being.

I had heard it all in hushed tones when I'd enter a room. I'd heard it from the mouths of people who were supposed to love me unconditionally for who I am, flaws and all, but they were the very people to pick up the pitchforks and set fire to everything I was until there wouldn't be a shred of my existence remaining on this earth. And if I was unfortunate enough to survive, there would be no piece left of me worth redeeming.

I had never given much thought about my life expectancy until I chose to live my life by my own rules—rules that no one approved or understood. I was a ticking time bomb living on borrowed time that no one believed was worth the risk of exile. No, that would have been too simple, too easy with no finality. And they were owed forever.

Death was a kindness in their eyes. They thought they were protecting everyone, that I would infect the herd. It was a catching, viral disease, and anyone could get it just by being in the same proximity as me. I watched as people recoiled or walked in the opposite direction the moment I caught their eye. They hid behind their God, praying for my family, praying that I'd see my way back to the path of the righteous before I let the needle prick my skin, but they were too late, like they'd always been. There was no saving me from this mutation.

Fallen twigs and branches snapped beneath my feet as I continued to push myself past the point of exertion, but it still felt like I was running in a circle. The further I got, the harder my father's prized blood runners, Maze and Rook, ran, eating up every inch I left in my wake. They'd been trained for this where I wasn't, and they had no other end goal than to run me down and pick at my bones, leaving nothing behind. I never liked them and for good reason. They were vicious and were never taught to coexist with anyone other than my father. My brothers and I knew better than to get near them or any of the other dogs our father owned—not even our momma liked them. But these two weren't simply meant for working around the ranch—no, they were meant to do irreparable damage to any threat, human or not.

I was the threat. Not only in this moment as I ran for my life, but to the Sorensen name, to the legacy my father had built. I'd become a risk they couldn't manage, the damage they couldn't mitigate. I stood to tarnish every bit of what the Sorensen name was built on. And Taylor Sorenson would not have it.

They'd given me enough rope to hang myself, and maybe I should have. It would have been the easiest option, but it wouldn't have been by my hand, whether it looked that way or not. Killing myself would have never been a one-man job no matter how they would have spun the story. Even if I stood solitary under the rafters on a chair with a noose around my neck ready to take the plunge, I could see each of them standing around me as plain as day.

As I conjured that very image in my mind, I wondered if a familiar pair of whiskey irises hidden beneath a black felt cowboy would be among them. Would he fan the flames? Or would he turn on them like they had done to me?

I didn't let myself hope on a normal day, but in this moment I hoped he would be the one demanding my innocence be proven. But like anything else in my life, I was never that lucky. Hope was a fool's death. It rotted its victim from the inside out, corrosive and intoxicating, until they're left with nothing. The world never stopped turning, passing them by while they stood still waiting for something or someone to tell them that their prayers had been answered, that they finally gave enough and now it would all be okay. It could bring the most devout man to his knees by masquerading as their Lord's will. I'd seen it so many times that I was incapable of having faith in things I couldn't see with my eyes or feel beneath my fingertips. Blind faith in any person other than myself was a fate I could never afford to succumb to, and I refused to, even for a man who had placed his faith and hopes in me. He trusted me to keep things he held close to his heart safe, hidden from prying eyes, but how could I keep him safe when I was being ripped open from stem to stern for simply choosing to live.

The more he cautioned me to wait, to bide my time, the more I pushed back, eviscerating myself in the barbed wire lining the ramparts meant to shackle me. He had good intentions, but how could he not see me drowning, that remaining as I'd always been would kill me faster than any punishment my father could dole out. If I remained as I was, we could have had it all, but it would always cost me more than I was willing to pay to have a taste of life with him. There was no way they would accept him back into the fold if they realized who I was, was not a deterrent but his preference. And if that realization came to light, I would not be the only one running.

Hope and good intentions were not going to save me. And neither was their God.

1

LEVI
EIGHT YEARS LATER

'Novocaine' Too Close To Touch, Bad Omens

I wouldn't say I'm stupid by any stretch of the imagination. I did make it this far without too many hiccups, but this was probably one of the shittier decisions I've made, getting in the car with Jameson when he's this emotional. Even if he wasn't wearing his emotions plain as day, I could feel them suffocating us.

Under any other circumstances, I'd trust Jameson implicitly. He'd been in my life ever since I set foot in Atlanta, whether I wanted him to be or not. He appointed himself my best friend, and the rest was history. But the more I dissected him, the more I was convinced befriending him would expose me. I didn't expect some uppity punk kid to be the heir to the Godfrey dynasty. The two of us would've never been in the same circles, simply because I refused to be involved in the upper crust bullshit, but our grandparents did, and that could've fucked me any day of the week. Somehow, it never happened.

The moment Onyx called him, I knew something had

happened, but it became abundantly clear how serious the situation was when Jameson's personal security, who he bulked against and refused to cooperate with, flooded his office and had his stepfather on the phone moments later. They bullied their way into Jameson's office with a half-cocked plan of getting Nyx out, but it was idiotic for them to believe anyone other than Jameson could get Nyx without so much as a hair out of place on either of their heads. Especially while Alessio was occupying that tomb of a house. Alessio was volatile on a good day, but when he was intentionally provoking Jameson…no one wanted to be around for that.

In the years I've known Jameson, I'd never seen him care about one of his boys before, but this boy was different for some reason I couldn't understand. He cared about him on a surface level that made Jameson a decent boss to work for, but this was above and beyond. Of course I didn't hate Nyx, but I wasn't going to go out of my way to save him from himself or the devil he'd invited into his life. Nyx was many things, but naïve wasn't one of them. And if he wanted to get in bed with one of the Kahn twins, that was on him entirely. After a warning from Jameson and myself, I thought he would steer clear of Alessio. I guess I was wrong in thinking he wasn't bullheaded. Even knowing who else might very well be in that house, I still got in the passenger seat as soon as Jameson hung up with his stepfather.

"What is it about this kid for you, Jameson?" I could have kept my mouth shut, but the question is out before I can stop myself.

His jaw clenches, the tendons bunching together so tight they look ready to snap from the pressure. Stress permeates the SUV as we smoothly navigate the streets of downtown Atlanta, and my question lingers in the air like a weighted balloon. If I had the capacity for it, I would empathize with him, but that's why Jameson and I would always be worlds apart. He cares so deeply for his people and would bend over backwards to make sure they're taken care of, and somehow Nyx had become one of those people like I had. I can't explain how it happened or even when it happened, but once Jameson decides you're his, there's no going back.

When he still doesn't answer the question, I peek at him again, hoping to see some indication of what he's thinking, but there isn't a single trace of emotion on his face any longer. The closer we get to his family estate, the less anyone would be able to see the real Jameson. He tucks those pieces of himself away until he's unrecognizable, and as easily as I'd grown used to it, it still pains me to see the God forsaken sunshine in him snuffed out so quickly just to survive.

I want to press him again, but it wouldn't do any good. Jameson has checked out. A heavy silence fills the SUV as Banks' "Judas" plays for the fifth time. My fingers itch to change the song to anything else, anything that wouldn't force me to reminisce and drown in memories of my life before Atlanta.

Even though I know it's nearly impossible to outrun who I was, I still fucking try. To this day I'm still running, and I don't know if I'll ever stop—which is a prime example as to why getting in the car with Jameson was a less than stellar decision on my part, but if I back out now, it would raise too many questions. Ones I have no intention of answering.

I know who's in that house with them. I'd served him countless times over the years when he was in town on business. I knew his order like the back of my hand. But I had never been more grateful for the choice to have minimal lighting at the bar than when I saw Cortland Thierry for the first time in five years, and he couldn't even recognize me—still couldn't. I'd watched him from a safe distance from behind the bar of the Fallout for the past three years without a single fuck up, and here I was walking into the belly of the beast without any way to disguise myself. Not a single person from home knew where I was, and I had fully intended to keep it that way, so Cortland knowing I'm in Atlanta will inevitably fuck everything up for me, and here I am helping the process along.

The further we stray from the city and into more residential areas, it becomes more desolate with the exception of a single streetlight I'd passed too many times to count, but every time I saw it, it felt like coming home...even when I refused to believe it was. Dense forest and winding roads have become a comfort to me again over the years, but it wasn't like that the first time Jameson brought me to his home. They were what I was used to growing up in Louisiana, and I wanted any reminder of that time to be erased. I hated it for so long, I gravitated toward the city to get away from anything that forced me to think of not only Cortland, but also my family. Jameson never questioned it, and to this day, he struggles with tamping down the impulse to pry. I feel it every time he looks at me, the hope that I will someday let him in. He had it in his head that once we'd grown as closely as we did, I would spill my guts to him or maybe even his mother, but it was the only thing keeping them at a comfortable distance for me.

After nearly a decade, they still have no idea who I was or where I came from, just that I needed help and was too much of a stubborn fuck to ask for it.

As grateful as I am for everything Dr. Godfrey had done for me, helping me transition and reshaping me without so much as batting an eye, I still hold myself apart from her and her son. They deserve better than what I am—a user. I know as sure as I'm sitting here next to Jameson as we near his family estate that's who I am at my core. I didn't have the heart to walk away from them when I should have then, and I don't have it now. It's too good—they are too good to me. And I am more than happy to wring out every drop of their generosity until it is an empty husk like I am. They are caring, attentive, and downright suffocating in a way that my family never was. Even Momma, bless her heart, tried to accept me, but it got too hard to see past what Daddy filled her head with; no one went against him. The damage he inflicted on her, in front of me and my brothers, when she deviated, if she hesitated for even a moment, was a cruelty she should have never experienced. While my brothers and I would take the brunt of his wrath without a second thought, we couldn't be there forever, and forcing her to fend for herself if she ever decided to leave him was never a choice I had the heart to force her to make. Momma might've loved all her children, but Daddy wasn't raised that way, and falling out of line with him was a mistake you'd die learning from if you were stupid enough to do it in the first place.

Respect was his currency, and I'd run poor when I was tired of living a lie to save my own skin.

The SUV comes to a crawling speed until we slow to a stop at the gate leading to the house. Jameson lets out a pained sigh, rolling down his window to talk to one of Alessio's men who is stationed outside. Seamlessly, Jameson slips into conversation with the man as if nothing was wrong, Russian spilling past his lips like it was second nature, and I guess it is because I'd had to learn as well to keep up with his family and staff who his stepfather had insisted on having round the clock. It just made my skin crawl being waited on hand and foot by people who didn't know me from Adam. Always "Mr. Reigns, this," and "Mr. Reigns, that," when I just wanted to be left alone and not be treated like an invalid.

They continue talking, but I tune it out until my ears involuntarily perk up with the mention of Cortland's name. When the gates finally open, I run through as many excuses as I can to stay in the damn car, but before I can open my mouth, Jameson beats me to it.

"I don't need to tell you what state we might find him in, but at least try not to pick a fight with Alessio regardless of what he's done. I'm not in the mood for your shit tonight. Can you handle that, Levi?" Jameson says, his voice devoid of emotion. He isn't expecting an answer, just that I'll obey. I know what we might walk into, and I have no qualms about keeping my mouth shut if Alessio does. In Jameson's defense, it's a nice idea but the wrong people to expect to follow his rules.

Jameson doesn't bother waiting for me to get out of the SUV as he trudged up the stairs, nearly ripping the front door off the hinges and slipping into the house. I'm not in a rush to follow him, taking my time to light a cigarette. Listening to Alessio try to charm his way out of being reprimanded seems more entertaining anyway.

Leaning back against the cool metal of the passenger door, I watch the breeze sweep up the smoke exiting my lungs and carry it off into the abyss of the night before settling my gaze on the house that nurtured me for years, only to find it more unfamiliar than the city had become. Vines from the overgrown foliage climb the aged white sandstone. Cracks spiderwebbed, fracturing the once pristine exterior where the foundation had begun to settle the same way Alessio and Jameson had splintered their parents' relationship that still hadn't recovered. Both were to blame, but Jameson did what he could to triage and remain obstinate while Alessio did everything in his power to wear his stepbrother down. But deep down we all knew what Jameson's actions after his parents found out what they were up to behind closed doors did to Alessio, and it was devastating. He loved Jameson in his own fucked up way, but it wasn't enough. That was one thing we had in common, much to our mutual displeasure.

I do my best to shake the thought from my head, taking one last drag before I stub out my cigarette on the bottom of my boot and flick it onto the hood of Alessio's car as I pass it and force myself to climb the stairs. Hopefully, Alessio drugged Nyx up enough so he wouldn't remember this shit. It was a fucked up thought, but it was better than the alternative. He'd been here for three hours, but fifteen minutes was all Alessio needed to inflict irreparable damage, physical or psychological, and as much as I didn't want to imagine what had been done, I still knew.

When I reach the front door, I see a glassy-eyed Nyx leaning against Cortland right inside the door in an all too familiar fashion that makes my blood boil. It isn't his fault he's so blitzed out of his mind that he needs help to remain upright, but it still doesn't piss me off any less.

Silently, I slither my way into the house undetected and settle against the wall of the entryway. I light another cigarette as I watch the scene unfold in front of me. Jameson yelling at Alessio for messing with one of his boys, Nyx grappling with trying to find some semblance of control, Cortland trying to soothe him in a way that makes my stomach roll. Alessio sprawling out in a chair is the picture of nonchalance as Jameson continues berating him about messing with his boys and going to their father about this, but the hearts swirling in Alessio's eyes as Jameson takes him apart is proof that this is all he wanted. He's struggling to hold himself back, the indecision is plain as day, but Jameson is too fired up to even see the adoration and lust aimed his way by his stepbrother. It's unbearably heartbreaking watching Alessio each time he's in the same room as Jameson, but no one says a word. Even his twin, Andreas, steers clear of them when they're near each other. It has gotten so bad that Jameson's friend Xander opened his home to him since

Alessio has been back in Atlanta for all of two weeks, and he's already wreaking havoc.

Jameson might be a pocket-sized twink, but his wrath is something to be reckoned with. He's always been tiny ever since I'd met him, and really, I wasn't sure how his very soft, very enlarged heart that was a sucker for basket cases and broken things could manage to fit in his lithe body, but it did.

One of Alessio's men grabs Jameson by the waist as he invades Alessio's space, and all hell breaks loose. Alessio wrenches the man's arm behind his back, pressing his body into the nearest pillar of the entryway and threatens his life. His tall, muscular frame dwarfs the man easily, and for a moment I think he's going to dislocate his arm from his shoulder, but Jameson simply places a hand on Alessio's back, soothing the beast prowling beneath the surface. A small whimper breaks my fixation on them, and I return my attention to Nyx and Cortland. The sight gnaws at the soft, gooey pieces of me that I'd buried deep many years ago, and the air around me thins as I watch it all unfold around me. But this time I can't break the tether between us as Cortland looks in my direction for just a split second. My breathing becomes shallow, and needles prickle along my flesh as I wait for him to say something, but he breaks the connection first.

All as I stood there like a fly on the wall, watching the man who haunted me each time my eyes grew heavy enough to pull me into the ether. Eight years has not been enough time, not when I would always crave even the slightest hint of his presence, his attention. Though I was no longer recognizable to the naked eye, I expected more than a dismissive flick of his whiskey irises, but I got nothing more than an irritating once over before he returned his attention to Nyx. I don't know why I expected more when every trace of Aubrey Sorensen had died, and for that I was grateful, but

Cortland's presence threatened the life I had sacrificed everything for.

"Nyx, come," I demand without an ounce of empathy for him. Nyx complies like an obedient dog, shrugging Cortland's weight off him and stumbling into my arms when he reaches me. I feel a sick sense of satisfaction that he's no longer touching Cortland. The momentary distraction allows one of Alessio's men to pull Cortland's attention away from us, giving me enough privacy to catalogue the damage they'd inflicted.

I lift Nyx's chin to get a look at his eyes, knowing with Alessio, it wasn't a party without favors, and I know Nyx already has a little bit of a problem. Blown pupils nearly overtake his irises, the blood vessels of his sclera screaming from stress, and I can almost guarantee there is hemorrhaging. He doesn't fight me while I check over the rest of his body, finding welts covering the back of his thighs and ass that leave little to the imagination of what else I might find beneath the scrap of clothes they dressed him in. If I had to guess, he'd been given a heavy cocktail of an upper and a downer, enough to make him compliant, agreeable even, and Alessio had the means.

I wonder which welts on his skin belonged to Cortland, what he had done to Nyx. I'm curious if Cortland was the one who broke him.

As Nyx's body sways into my own, the overwhelming scent of Cortland's sweat and piss coats the back of my tongue. Onyx dissolves in my arms the moment I'm not holding him up, and I can't help but bury my nose in the delicate slope of his neck. I inhale deeply, getting high off the scent embedded in his flesh. I catch my breath, only to do it again, making Nyx shiver in my arms. A choked moan escapes him as my fingers bite into his battered skin, his cock brushing against my thigh that was meant to be holding him steady, but he chases the friction a little too eagerly, and I break the connection.

Jameson glances in our direction before turning his attention back to his brother, chastising him in front of his men. When I hear Jameson drop Cortland's name with a familiarity he shouldn't have, shock takes over my body, and I want to do the only thing I'm good at—run. It's the second time tonight Jameson has carelessly mentioned a man's name that he should have no connection to whatsoever. I watch closely as Cortland joins their already heated discussion, my insides quivering as the familiar cadence of his gravelly, baritone voice swamps my auditory cortex. I let myself seek him out once more, using Nyx as a shield but also to ground me in place, keeping me stationary.

Even though I'd seen him more than a handful of times in recent years, it wasn't like this. Cortland is every bit of the man I had imagined he would be. Aged like fine fucking wine. He's as imposing as he had ever been, but he sticks to the shadows, keeping attention diverted elsewhere, which is not the man I had known him to be. Maybe it was the hero worship that warped my image of him as a child, but there was something missing—something that had been taken from him. I couldn't put my finger on it, not that he would want anyone to.

I ache to run my fingers through the stubble lining his sharp jawline. I want to feel the roughness of it against my tongue and commit his taste to memory. I want to tug on the sandy blonde hair hidden under his black cowboy hat, to hear him hiss and groan under the pressure. The thought of it alone makes my dick hard as moisture seeps from my hole, drenching my briefs. And fuck if I'm not tempted to wrap myself around his leg and worship his filthy Lucchese boots until my cum soils them further and my inner thighs chafe from the leather while he shoves my face into his crotch, holding me there and forcing me to inhale his sweaty musk after a long day of riding. It's disgusting and shameful, the things I want him to do to me, but I can't get myself to stop, and I don't care. I want it all.

The wayward fantasy comes to a screeching halt the moment he reaches up to adjust the brim of his hat. It is a completely innocent tick that I had always loved, one I was used to, but a simple adornment on his left ring finger makes me want to crawl into the shallow grave Alessio has threatened me with a time or two. I want—no, *need*—it to be fake. There is no conceivable way that it could be true, that he could have married *her*. Not after everything we talked about on that last summer night together in the bayou. It just couldn't be. How I completely missed it the countless times he'd sat across from me at the bar, I have no idea.

No matter how many times I blink, hoping that I am seeing things, it remains firmly soldered to his finger. The worn metal isn't leaving my sight as if it's taunting me, laughing at me, telling me that I had been a stupid fucking kid. And clearly, I had been. I was so goddamn naive to believe him, to have given him something so precious so many years ago. I kept my mouth shut and left because I no longer had a choice, but he had stayed, stayed, and married that fucking girl.

An ugly laugh escapes my throat, pulling everyone's attention towards me—including his. Cortland finally takes a long look at what he can decipher between me and Nyx, who is still plastered against me, before his gaze settles on the one thing that I could never change no matter how many times Dr. Godfrey tried.

There is no denying who I am now that he's seen the scar that Cortland himself stitched up while feeding me Banamine to help subside the excruciating pain. Really, I had gotten lucky, but in that moment, no one could have told me that. It had been a freak accident, but I would never forget the terror that I saw in Cortland's eyes when I got my bearings enough to pick myself up off the ground and all he could see was my face covered in blood.

The scar served as a reminder that even placing your trust implicitly in things that you had grown and nurtured from their inception could cost you more than you had ever bargained for.

We remained frozen, both staring at each other until I break the tether holding us together for so long. One I should have severed the moment I left Louisiana, and him, in my rearview.

"Come on, Nyx. It's time for us to go." I rouse him enough to loosen his grip on me before pulling him towards the door.

Regrettably, the only way to leave brings me closer to Cortland, who looks pained the closer I get to the door, before I force our way past him and into the chill of the night. As I struggle to get Nyx into the backseat of Jameson's SUV, I feel him before I see him. I knew he'd follow me, like he always did. If I moved, he moved, like I still held his strings, and he was my beautiful marionette to manipulate any way that I pleased.

The moment I close the door of the SUV, sealing Onyx inside, I relax my weight against Cortland like I had so many times before, and his less than sure arms come to band around my waist, his warmth surrounding me. He made it so easy to forget.

"Cort."

The single word, the name he'd let me call him, breaks his resolve and his arms tighten around me. A choked sound, almost like a sob, meets my ears and startles me, but it also makes me smile. His cries have always been my favorite. His eyes, red-rimmed and glossed with tears, make his irises shimmer, brightening the usual whiskey color to a honey brown that I want to see for the rest of my life. But the most intoxicating thing about him is the way he smells, almost as good as he tasted. It hasn't changed a bit: cherries, dark chocolate, and tobacco. It was overpowering, so masculine and rich.

Cortland buries his face in the juncture of my throat and inhales deeply as if to familiarize himself with my scent all over again, but smelling me had not been the goal. His heated tongue meets my flesh and travels up to my earlobe, which he sucks into his mouth. I squirm against him, his hands squeezing my hips to the point of pain, and a whimper works its way past my lips when the hard length of his cock grinds into my crease.

His calloused hand shoves its way into my pants and briefs with practiced ease before finding my cock already pulsing with need for him. Cortland slots his middle and forefinger on either side my cock, just like I had shown him, and starts stroking my hardened flesh in an agonizingly slow pace that sets my soul on fire.

"Vi, fuck." My knees threaten to buckle the moment my name leaves his lips. The addicting scent of his breath assaults my senses as his teeth latch onto the sensitive skin of my jaw. Cinnamon gum and Marlboro red cigarettes—my favorite combination.

"Long time, no see, cowboy." I moan, nearly tripping over the childhood nickname I had given him.

A dark laugh rumbles against my back, and I squirm and writhe in Cortland's arms the longer he toys with me. He sinks his thick fingers inside me, stretching me to the point of pain. The burn is delicious. I gasp as his fingers curl and press against the front wall of my hole, adding increasing pressure to my urethra until I feel the embarrassing urge to piss all over his hand—fuck, he's going to kill me, and I haven't even had a chance to taste him again. I haven't even savored him the way I had always meant to.

Cold metal pinches my sensitized flesh and yanks me back down to earth. The blinding pain makes me want to scream. It's not even a physical pain; the single pinch was nothing for me to endure. What I can't fathom is that he is here with me in his arms, but he couldn't be any less mine than he had always been. As quickly as I had fallen into him again, it was easily ripped away.

I struggle to get out of his arms, forcing him to let me go. My breathing becomes more ragged as panic sets in and wraps around my nervous system, choking my cognitive abilities until I double over. Cortland scrambles to catch me as my knees crack against the unforgiving pavement but seems to think better of it before he can make contact. He takes a step back, giving me the space I need but that I want less than anything. And I don't know if that makes it worse or if it should have been a relief, but it brings tears to my eyes anyway.

"Levi, what's wrong?" He asks, his voice no longer feeling like a comfort. I shake my head, refusing to answer him.

I don't want to explain it; it wouldn't make fucking sense. None of it did. I was angry with him for doing the same thing that I had done. We chose survival over each other, and I am making the same decision now. It didn't hurt so bad when I didn't know. It was easier to conjure up any other outcome that he could have chosen, but I knew deep in my bones that he had gone through with it and married Diana if for no other reason than to end the vitriol between him and his father, and I couldn't fault him for it, but fuck, if it doesn't feel like the air has been ripped from my lungs.

I need Jameson to hurry up and stop fucking around with his brother. I need to be able to breathe. I need.

Minutes tick by before he reaches for me again, and I can't suppress the instinct to recoil, backing away from his touch. Neither of us says another word while I pull myself together and finally stand. I lift my gaze to find him already looking at me, hurt etched into his beautiful face. Honeyed eyes stare back at me as I lean into the cold metal door of the SUV to support my weight and to keep me from crumbling in front of him again. It is all I can do to keep myself controlled, to stop myself from giving in and letting myself fall to pieces.

It would be so easy to seek refuge in him, but as much as I want to, I won't. I can't let myself fall into that trap.

"Why are you even here?" I ask, genuinely curious, but I don't know if I want the answer if he's tied up with Alessio on some level.

"Business. Has this been where you've chosen—"

I scoffed, cutting him off before he could finish the question. A strained laugh comes out while I take a few seconds to stare at him. "Don't ask questions if you're not going to be forthcoming. We never lied to each other so unless you plan to tell me what you were doing in his house, we don't need to do this. You shouldn't have followed me out here in the first place."

Cortland eyes the SUV I'm leaning against before shaking his head. If he was anyone else in his position, I would have let it go and chalked it up to him being here solely for Nyx at Alessio's request, but that's not what this was. Alessio wasn't someone you just partied with randomly without an invitation, but I'd seen them together on multiple occasions over the years, silently watching Cortland from afar. I'm not ready to show my hand, but I also am not willing to budge on needing to hear it from him. I want to hear it in his own words, how he managed to get in with the bratva if he was simply a rancher. There was no correlation or reason I can formulate myself that makes sense.

"We're goin' to have this conversation whether you like it or not, Levi. Did you think I would just let you walk away after I saw you?" He takes a step closer, bringing himself a little too close for comfort. Too close to touch when my fingers are itching to feel his skin against mine.

"Honestly? Yes, Cortland, I did. What good would it do? Besides, if we hadn't seen each other tonight, another decade would've gone by, and you would be none the wiser." I'm being heartless, and I know it. I'd had eyes on him for years without him knowing. I shake my head, a grin starts pulling at my lips but I fight it, just to twist the knife deeper, "Besides, you just fucked Nyx because Alessio provided his new toy to be passed around for this evening entertainment. Clearly you have no qualms being the whore you've always been."

"You really believe that horseshit, don't you?" A tremor in his cadence softens me, but I can't bring myself to show him even the slightest weakness I still have for him.

"Oh, God. What else am I supposed to believe? That you've been pining for me after all this time? That you still hold out hope for us?" I fake a pout, looking up at him for a moment and softening my eyes until tears welled up just enough before letting it fall away again. "No, I don't believe that. We both moved on, didn't we?" My eyes settle on his wedding band, forcing him to acknowledge its existence for the first time since he followed me out here.

"When did you become so cold?" The insecurity in his voice begins to bleed through, but it isn't my responsibility to console him anymore.

"Oh, sweetie, I always was. I just never had a reason to be less than the doting little girl who followed you around from the time that I knew what it meant to want the wrong person." The venom saturating my words and sickening grin tugging at my lips forces him to take a step back from me until he's no longer within striking distance.

It is only made unbearable by the way he looks at me. The same way he looked at his father.

2

CORTLAND

'Different Man' Kane Brown, Blake Shelton

Somehow, I am supposed to reconcile with the idea that the person who is standing in front of me is the same person that I'd been trying to get back to for longer than I'd care to admit.

When Levi disappeared after announcing to his father he's a man, it was like he no longer existed. No one talked about him, and if anyone did and his father heard about it, the world stopped. It took me a few years to find him, but I chose not to interfere and as many times as I told myself I never would, it was a lie. His exile was devastating, the pain of losing him without so much as a goodbye or even a note haunted me but I couldn't bring myself to disturb the peace I thought he found.

I kept tabs on him after meeting Alessio while I was in Vegas for PBR. How Levi was connected to Alessio didn't make any sense to me at the time, but when Alessio introduced me to Jameson, his stepbrother and Levi's best friend, the pieces slowly started to fall into place. Finding him behind the bar of Jameson's club threw me for a loop and it took every ounce of restraint I had to remain a stranger to him.

As many times as I sat across from Levi while at Fallout, I was still shocked. The man standing only feet away from me is anything but what I expected to find. Levi is no longer the gangly kid who hid beneath clothes that were three sizes too big for him, or stole his brothers beaten to death jeans held up by a belt and a prayer. He is striking, and anything but what I expected to find after a decade apart. Tattoos crawl up his neck, encasing the column of his throat like a collar with a stark negative space in center. A metal bar flashes between his teeth with each word he speaks while the moonlight gleans from the one through his eyebrow and the stud in his nostril. He traded his cowboy boots for combat boots and his flannel-lined jean jacket for a leather jacket that was painted on his skin, hugging the muscle he'd put on.

He isn't my Levi anymore. He is something else entirely.

"Are you just going to stare at me like I'm a circus freak, or are you going to say what you have to say, Cortland?" His voice slices through the pregnant silence that has fallen between us, snapping me out of the daze I find myself in the longer I stay in his orbit.

I force myself to rein in the impulse to grab him the way I want to when he continues to lash out like the brat he is. He absolutely isn't mine to punish, but that doesn't mean I would stand here and listen to him spout off at the mouth without correcting him. I hate every minute of this. I hate that he wasn't mine. But more than anything, I hated the glaring distance between us that I have no way of repairing.

"What did I tell you about that attitude of yours? If you want to keep speakin' freely, I suggest you fix it, boy." I grind out through gritted teeth, barely holding onto the shred of control I have left.

"And if I don't?" He lifts a brow in my direction, challenging me. His head tilts to the side, his unruly onyx curls falling across his forehead as he studies me, dissecting me until my skin crawls. It's unnerving how detached he's become, so cold and lifeless. He gives nothing away while he pulls a cigarette out with his teeth and flicks his lighter, the flame dancing in front of his face. When I don't give him an answer as fast as he would like, his agitation makes him reckless enough to get close to me again, blowing the smoke in my face as he continues to taunt me. "This is getting tiresome. Will you, won't you..." He sighs dramatically, "Really, Cortland? Not going to threaten me?" He pouts again, before a predatory grin disfigures his beautiful face.

"You're more than welcome to test that theory, but before you do, because we both know you can't help yourself..." I take the few steps needed to back him into the door of the SUV again, ignoring the burning cherry searing into my skin as his cigarette swipes across my jaw, and whisper in his ear, "Remember that I was the one who taught your skin to sing."

With those parting words, I walk back into the house and past Jameson, who is still making Alessio feel like the red-headed stepchild he is. Pain in the ass that he is, Alessio wasn't the worst that I'd dealt with but a necessary evil when it came time to get out from underneath Marcus' control over my family and the ranch. It had been a process, a fucking long one, but I needed to protect every bit of what I'd built without the slightest margin for error. Nothing could slip through the cracks. But these trips back and forth left me wide open. It left my family unprotected. A business could be rebuilt, but the family I'd created couldn't be.

Diana knew something was going on. She'd been on board from day one when I came to her telling her that I wanted out, out of the arena, out of our sham of a marriage. We did what we both had to, to survive living in a state so deeply indoctrinated in intolerance. We may have love for each other, but that didn't happen overnight nor did what we built together.

My phone begins to ring, pulling me from my thoughts, and when I check my caller ID, a grin spreads across my face. Nightly FaceTime calls with Elliott made leaving for a week at a time worth every bit of the turmoil it could cause.

His little face fills the screen, although it was mainly a shot of his messy, wet blonde hair because even though we'd done this countless times, he still doesn't understand that he needs to back up from the camera.

"Bubba, he can't see your face when you have the screen that close to you." Diana tries to explain for what feels like the thousandth time. She lets out a sigh that ended in a breathy laugh as he starts to lower the tablet from over his head.

"You givin' your Momma trouble, son?" I ask in the sternest voice he rarely hears from me.

He turns to look at me with owlish eyes, the same way he had when he got caught in the stallion barn alone when we first started having him in lessons. It was a scare that neither Diana nor myself had been prepared for. Even though our stallions were well behaved, all it would take for one of them to send Elliott running was them smelling one of our broodmares in flaming heat, which at the time was happening regularly during breeding season, but Elliott hadn't understood that quite yet. After that, he steered clear of the stallion barn unless it was out of season or one of us was with him to tack up.

As much as people love to say their horses are bomb proof, having a stallion near a mare in heat was always a risk, and keeping Elliott safe was our top priority, one that wasn't afforded to either of us as kids.

His head bobs up and down in a choppy nod before he

answers my question and makes my heart soften. "Of course not, Daddy. I'm holdin' down the fort just like you made me promise. We shook on it, remember?"

"Yeah, and what else did we promise? Do you remember what we said?"

With all the seriousness he could muster, he stiffened his upper lip and straightened up before reciting exactly what I had said. "Mhm. You said that while you were gone that I was the man of the house, and that Momma would need me to be on my very best behavior because she'd be worryin' herself sick until you came home, and that if anythin' happened to you, Momma needs to call Mr. Reigns and tell him that 'moonshine in the bayou made every eight worth it.' And that no matter what you love me." His eyes brighten, and he gives me a gummy smile when he finishes. It's the same thing I tell him every time I leave.

A throat clears, pulling my attention from my son only to see the last person I want to be bothered with—Jameson. He fills the doorway of the kitchen and remains motionless until I return my focus to Elliot. He slinks past me while my son rambles on about wanting to spend more time with his colt that we'd recently started under saddle before I'd left. Diana wasn't too pleased about Elliott starting on a colt that hadn't been gelded because of the potential bad outcome even if he was good minded, but Ares was his.

"That's right, Elliott. Never forget it." He beams at me like he'd won a contest at the county fair and was about to get the biggest stuffed animal he could manage to carry. I regret shattering our little bubble, but the words are out before I can stop them, not having a choice in the matter. "Listen, Daddy has to go, but I love you no matter what, and I'll be home soon. If you listen to your Momma, we'll take Ares out for some miles under saddle."

"Cortland, I will be damned if you put my son on that

damn stallion. Don't you da—" I hang up before she can get the rest of her sentence out. She hates the notion that Elliott wants to be a rider, even though it was bred into him from both of us. We couldn't keep him away from the horses if we wanted to. She would just have to get over it.

"What is it, Jamie?" I snap at him without bothering to turn around.

"Oh, nothing." He huffs dramatically. He continues to buff his nails on the fabric of his too expensive shirt before checking them again. The sound of a hangnail snagging on the fabric is too much like nails on a chalkboard, and it takes everything in me to ignore his presence. "Cute kid. Shame his daddy prefers the company of whores rather than his own wife."

"If you want to keep your tongue, don't mention my son to me ever again, Jameson. Are we clear?" I was tired of his incessant games every time we were in the same room, and he knew it.

"Crystal. But tell me something, yeah? You've known he was here all this time, didn't you? You didn't need me or Alessio to figure that out." It isn't meant as a question so much as an accusation.

In for a penny, in for a pound.

"I have always known exactly where he is, and who's been watching over him, otherwise I wouldn't have left him alone for as long as I have. I made the choice not to interfere if he was safe and breathing, which you have seemed to manage over the years. But the better question is how long have you known who I was and why keep it from him this long?"

When he doesn't answer immediately, I turn around to find him leaning against the marble counter, and he can't seem to look at me. It clicks. Jameson was never supposed to know anything about Levi that he hadn't told him. That he was never supposed to know about me. I should have seen it coming, but it doesn't dull the pain that lances through my chest. Nearly ten years was ample time to learn particulars about someone, and Jameson didn't learn the slightest thing about who Levi was from Levi.

Levi didn't want to remember, and I have to accept that.

"Don't look at me like that, Cortland." He snaps, his voice cracking like a whip.

"I'm not lookin' at you any kinda way, kid. For someone who knows him as well as I do, I'm sure you more than understand how he will react when he finds out. And it won't be me to tell him. I don't need to. But you're sorely mistaken if you think he won't put the pieces together eventually after seeing me here of all places. He's never been stupid, and if you're betting that he'll forgive you, you have another thing comin'."

I didn't have the intention to provoke him, but it doesn't surprise me when he tries to push me against the counter and get in my face. I stifle the urge to laugh at the ridiculous notion that Jameson could overpower me, yet him trying makes me feel slightly better that it is him who has been in Levi's corner all these years.

"Like you repeatedly coming into my club without your wedding band on and dangling yourself in front of him for the past few years? Did you think I wouldn't figure out who you were after months of you coming in just to make eyes at my bartender? Hmm?"

"Your bartender, huh? Is that a fact?" A gruff, broken chuckle leaves my throat as I force him to back up, plastering him against the opposite counter before thinking better of it. Something about hearing him reduce Levi just doesn't fucking sit right with me. His eyes widened slightly as if taking me in for the first time. "Does he know that's how you refer to him when he's not around? Like a piece of property, nothin' more than a number on your payroll? Or maybe he's the family dog? Yeah, that sounds about right for your kind. Tell me somethin', Jamie, how long did it take you to rehabilitate such a reactive animal and turn him into a loyal beast? Although, you didn't train it all out of him, did you? No, you weren't capable of handling him properly, and that much is clear."

"You have a lot of nerve. You don't know the first thing about me." He snarls as he tries to push his way out of my hold.

"I don't hear a denial. But hey, I understand wanting a return on your investment." I empathize and pat his cheek a little harder than necessary to keep his focus. "Now be a good boy, and tell me where he went tonight."

STALKING IS A STRONG WORD. It felt like when Momma would say 'hate' is a strong word just to replace it with saying dislike, which never encompassed the same feeling. I knew what I was doing was frowned upon, but stalking implied that the other person wouldn't appreciate being watched. This was the disillusion that led to me borrowing one of Alessio's cars and finding myself at an illegal car meet where Levi would be the night I was supposed to be boarding my plane to go back to Louisiana. I was so far out of my depth, but I wanted to put eyes on Levi before going home. If this is what he replaced riding with, I wanted to see it. I needed to know.

The music pulses, ricocheting off the pavement and bouncing between the silos, seeking impact as the smell of burning rubber fills the air. Swarms of bodies, an easy hundred, flock to two cars spinning dead center and locked on each other. Girls hanging out of car windows as they whip across the pavement, tires squealing as loud as the girls were. When Jameson said it wasn't safe, he didn't elaborate, but experiencing it is vastly different. If either driver fucks up for even a split second, the wreckage would kill not only the drivers but the people flooded around them creating a pit.

One of the car models I recognize from seeing it on the road so often, whether a cop or civilian drove it, but the other I couldn't even tell you the manufacturer name. Both seamlessly switch into what looks like a floating figure eight. Neither car spins out, and I cringe waiting for the impact of one or both, but it never comes.

They continue like that, leaving me in a daze until the rev of an engine that rivals the music snaps me back into focus, and I finally exit the car to work my way through the crowd. The possibility of Levi seeing me hasn't crossed my mind, but I know I would stick out like a sore thumb if I don't at least attempt to blend in. Although it wouldn't have made a difference if I hadn't gotten out of the damn car, yet here I was.

A sleek black Dodge Charger pulls up slower than I'm sure the driver intended, forcing the crowd to allow them into the circle that formed around the first two cars. Without making everyone wait too much longer as the song switches over, a Nissan of some sort ushers everyone out of the way only for the circle to close again. The driver in the Charger rolls his window and waits for the other driver to do the same. Impatiently, the first driver drums his finger along the driver side mirror with an indignant smirk on his face, almost baring his teeth in frustration of being ignored. After a moment, he gets out of the car and bangs on the window. No one moves, the music doesn't stop, and the window remains firmly in place.

Every onlooker in the growing crowd remains rooted in

place, and tension fills the air. As the window rolls down, smoke bellows out, and I shake my head. Levi. Always such a fucking brat.

"Reigns, get out of the fucking car," the guy bites out through gritted teeth. My eyes sink closed, knowing the animosity is warranted if Levi had anything to do with it. A fight is the last thing I accounted for, much less one that Levi would be involved in. As much as I want to rip into this guy for even slightly posing a threat to Levi, I can't.

Of course, Levi doesn't help the situation when he intentionally flicks the butt of his cigarette at the guy, making him scramble to keep from getting burned, earning a few rakish laughs from the crowd that had gravitated to the two of them.

"I'm perfectly comfortable right where I am, Woods. Why don't you get back in your car, so you don't hurt yourself, huh?" From the angle where I stand, I can't see his face, but I'd bet my bottom dollar that he is grinning. I can make out the flare of Woods' nostrils before he leans forward with his forearms resting on the roof of Levi's car. Woods lips are moving, a nasty snarl overtaking his features, and whatever he says pulls a visceral reaction from Levi. The combination of the crowd and the music make it impossible to hear the conversation, but Levi snatches Woods up by his collar, yanking him through the window, and all hell breaks loose. Fucking kids.

Levi hasn't seen me yet, and I should take this as an opportunity to split, but the idea of someone hurting Levi forces my body into action before I even realize what I'm doing. It's instinctive. It always has been. Before I even think it through, I'm pushing myself through the throng of overheated bodies to get to Levi.

By the time I reach Levi's car, Woods is screaming, and I see a flash of silver. It's an ear-piercing yet guttural sound like a horse when they scream out in pain, a sound I am too familiar with. I manage to pull Woods out of the driver's side window by the back of his shirt before Levi can inflict any more damage, although I'm sure he deserves it. He attempts to right himself with the momentum but still ends up splayed out on his back on the asphalt. I would have thought he was only wincing from having the wind knocked out of him if it weren't for the precise gash marring the right side of his face. When I look up to check on Levi, there isn't a scratch on him apart from his shirt being torn to shit.

"You better not let me get my hands on you, Reigns. You fucking fa—" I cut Woods off before he can finish spewing his vitriol toward Levi. I grab his jaw, applying an unnecessary amount of pressure when he tries to jerk out of my hold, enough to make it unhinge until I feel the bones and ligaments pop.

"Son, I don't suggest finishin' that sentence if you don't want to end up lookin' like the Joker." I snarl, my spit landing on his bloody face. Levi hadn't been too far off from completely fucking this kid's face up. A deep almost gaping laceration about four inches long is bleeding profusely from the corner of his mouth. Honestly, it looks exactly like he'd been caught in the mouth by a fishing hook and strung up to show off the catch of the day.

Levi snorts, "He really could smile more. Might make it easier to stomach dealing with him."

"Shut the fuck up, Levi." That mouth on him is exactly what got him into this, and it for damn sure is not doing us any favors now. His eyes flare with unmistakable rage when I meet his gaze, but the way his lids become the slightest bit heavy and the miniscule change in his breathing, hitching at my brash tone tell a different story altogether.

He doesn't miss a beat, though. "And why the hell are you here, Cortland? Couldn't leave well enough alone, could you?

I mean this is frankly just sad, you following me around like a lost puppy."

A grunt escapes the kid when I release my hold on him and let him hit the ground again to give Levi my full attention. Even with his shirt ruined, he still looks as unbothered as he always does. He doesn't ruffle easily, always so fucking steady that it would piss anyone off if they weren't used to it. Often it would make me angrier at a situation that was already sending my blood pressure through the roof. He's a port in the storm—a haven even when he thrived in the chaos. He reveled in it, taking a mile for every inch you gave him without hesitation.

I take a moment to pull myself together as he exits his car, watching as he unfolds himself from its confines. My tongue sticks to the roof of my mouth as I take in the leather molding to the muscles of his legs all the way down to the combat boots laced up his ankles. The ripped shirt leaves an endless road map of the tattoos littering his torso and chest on display. Too many to be able to focus on only one, except the one that caught my attention earlier. The blank space at his throat encased by intricate black ink on either side of the flawless pale skin that I want nothing more than to sink my teeth in.

Even a saint would have trouble keeping his hands to himself, and I'd bet money that Levi knew exactly what he did to men and women alike. He was arresting to witness doing the simplest things, but seeing him in his element feels like striking a match and lighting a fire in my veins I had no hope of extinguishing.

The smugness as he caught me looking at him longer than I'd allowed myself to any other time we'd been in each other's vicinity confirmed those thoughts. He knew and had no intention of ever making life easier on a single soul who became enraptured by him.

"Showing up in places you don't belong is gonna get you sent back home in a pine box if you keep this up, cowboy. When are you going to learn that you aren't welcome here, hm?" Levi warns as he leans back against his car without a care in the world for the fucker laying at his feet. It should not shock me that he doesn't have any qualms about threatening me or inflicting pain on someone without batting an eye, but it does. I really don't know him anymore–or maybe I do, and I chose to ignore it when it was never directed at me.

"You're right. Handle it yourself."

I don't miss the way his face falls even if it's just for a split second before he schools his features. There's no guilt when I walk away from him like I'd always imagined there would be, even though I'd been riddled with it for years on his behalf. I wasn't one to back down, especially when it came to him, but I find myself doing it for a second time. Yet this time I don't hesitate. The man standing in front of me is not who I'd been endangering my family for, sacrificing so many things for, but I might have to admit it wasn't worth it, and I'm not ready for that version of reality. The idea of Levi being anything other than the man I'd fallen in love with keeps my feet moving.

Even when he shouts at my back several things that might be true, but he's shown his hand without realizing it—he still wants me here.

3
LEVI

'The Machine — Slowed' Reed Wonder, Aurora Olivas

A few days passed since I saw Cortland walk away from me, and I thought I'd have been more used to it by now after watching him do it my whole life, but it created a different sensation when he did it intentionally like he had the other night. I'd also assumed he had gone back to his wife after that, and by God I wished he had. But no, he's sitting across from me at my bar, sipping my whiskey without a care in the world. Like we were old friends when we were anything but. I'd thought about banning him from Fallout many times over the years, but again, it would raise too many questions.

Cortland has made it very clear who he was here for. And everyone seemed to notice.

"Don't look so glum, Levi. He's hot as fuck, and he's clearly here for you," one of my coworkers said.

"Who pissed in your corn flakes this morning, Vi?" Fucking not Cortland, or I might've been happier.

It's starting to pluck my last nerve watching everyone fall

all over him, and who could blame them? I mean, seriously. He was like watching all your cowboy and southern gentleman fantasies jump off the pages of the latest trashy romance novel that everyone gushed about. He was the fantasy. Although to him, it was just his life, and it used to be mine too, no matter how many times I try to forget it.

"When are you returning home to your wife?" I ask, raising my voice just loud enough for my coworkers to do a double take. His eyes flash to mine, and he cocks an eyebrow, goading me, but I don't bother. At least some of the girls have the decency to look guilty for the way they'd been laying all over him. While most of them were dancers, the stereotype of dancers not caring if you have a wife and kids at home did not apply to them. I was used to seeing him get dances while he was here, but this was different. He'd come in here without wearing that Godforsaken wedding ring like he had many times before, but this time I knew, and I could see the tan line. It was a slap in the face every time I saw it now, and it had become impossible to ignore.

"When I get what I came for." I wasn't expecting an answer, but my body relaxes a bit at his words, although I have no clue what he means—his voice just has that effect on me. Whether he meant me or business, I didn't care.

Ignoring him, I go back to wiping down the already clean bar and lose myself in the music. His eyes never leave me. Not when I'm talking to clients as they come by before leaving for the night. Not as each waitress comes to place an order for a table. Not while I'm mixing drinks and closing tabs. But when someone gets a little too comfortable in their drunkenness, his eyes sharpen on them waiting for them to overstep. Like a goddamn reaper. People eye him warily each time he shifts closer to me, but he remains in his seat silently while he nurses his whiskey.

Nyx meanders over before his set and boldly strikes up a

conversation with Cort like he wasn't just trapped in a dungeon with the man. Dungeon might be dramatic, but for all intents and purposes that is what Alessio created for his little toys. I keep my distance, sneaking glances in their direction while still taking care of the few tabs that trickle in. It shouldn't bother me, but it does anyway. Nyx is beautiful whether he's clad in skimpy leather like he is now or falling all over himself because he's in too deep. Cort continues giving him his undivided attention like I don't exist, and something nasty sinks into my bones when he laces his fingers through Nyx's. His thumb softly caresses the back of his hand, and Nyx blushes at his words—words I can't fucking hear, but if I had to guess they were ones I'd heard before. It goes on for a few minutes before it hits me square in the chest.

Nyx doesn't remember.

I should feel bad for him, really, I know I should, but I can't find it in me to care.

Nyx chose to take on Alessio as a client, knowing what he might endure and if he doesn't want to be roofied for other people's amusement for the night, Nyx, himself, is the only one who can change the rules. While Alessio will take advantage of every inch someone gives him, he wouldn't if they told him no. Except for Jameson.

It's not that I would wish Alessio's attention upon anyone, Nyx included, but we warned him. Jameson explicitly told him to stay away from Alessio, and while Jameson has his own reason, I do too. Nyx is too good for this place, and he's too good to be Alessio's newest toy. What arrangement they had, we don't know, but it's never a topic of conversation. Not for me and Jameson, and surely not between him and Nyx. It had been a few days since we picked up Nyx from Alessio's, and Jameson was nowhere to be found. Unlike Cortland, who won't leave me alone and has been sitting at my bar every night, intentionally goading me, since he realized who I was. As much as I acted like I didn't want him around, I'm not ready for him to go home either. Not when I knew he'd be going back home to a woman who he'd married and had a little family with this entire time while I'd been alone.

Deep down I knew I wasn't alone, but no one filled the void he'd left inside of me and hell I tried. I heard what people said about me, and I didn't correct them. As I watched Nyx's finger trace the brim of Cortland's hat, I could conjure up the bodies who'd tried to comfort me over the years just as sure as anything. I never knew them outside of what they could do to my body and what I could do to theirs, and that's what we'd agreed upon. Sure, there had been a few here and there who I knew in my day-to-day life, but I quickly realized that I was better off not getting involved with someone who wanted more from me than I could offer.

Cortland would be disgusted if he knew what and who I'd been fucking while he was playing house. Nyx smiled at something else Cortland said and tried to appear demure or whatever the hell he was doing with his face when he wanted someone to take him up on the offer for a private room. Shy. Demure. Innocent. Doe-eyed.

Things I wasn't and would never be. I wasn't so insecure that I would ever mold myself into something I would never be, but seeing them like that, how easily they could just be, made me feel like I was never what Cortland truly wanted, and a pretty, little wife would always be his first choice.

As if he knew I was thinking of him, he looked me dead in the eyes over Nyx's shoulder. He gave me one of his winning smiles that I'd only seen a handful of times, and those smiles threatened to stop my heart every time. Of course, it could be played off like he was smiling at something stupid Nyx had said to him, but I know that smile is all for me, from the crow's feet crinkling around his eyes to the way that blinding smile fades into smugness before he winks and takes a swig of his whiskey.

The music switches over from one of the girls' sets coming to an end, and the moment I hear the first notes of SG Lewis' song "Warm," it feels like all the air in my lungs evaporates like fresh rain beating down in the bayou under the scorching sun. The sensuous beat lulls through the humid suffocating atmosphere of pheromones and body heat mixed with the scent of stale alcohol and citrus wafting up my nostrils. I need to get out of here. I can't listen to this song on my best day, but hearing it while he has eyes on me, while we are breathing the same air feels like a cruelty even I can't withstand.

I wave down Blaise before I think better of it. Confusion dances in his eyes when he notices my antsy demeanor but without questioning it, he tells the client across from him to hold on for a moment before making his way over to me like he would any other day. I appreciate him not making a scene by rushing over, though I wish he would for just a moment get some urgency in his step, but that just isn't who Blaise was. He moves to the beat of his own drum and is never in a rush for anyone.

"I need you to take the rest of my shift tonight and for the next couple of days." I rush out as soon as he is in ear shot. He arches a brow and begins opening his mouth to say something but thinks better of it.

"Are we good?" He asks, glancing over his shoulder to look at Cortland and Nyx before looking back at me. He knows something's up but still, he doesn't pry.

I nod even though we both know damn well I'm lying through my teeth. "Yeah, I just need a couple days to myself. Personal reasons."

"Vi, I know we don't—" I cut him off before he can get the rest of his words out with a wave of my hand.

"You're right, we don't. And we're not starting now. We're good. I need a couple days. If you need anything, call Jameson."

I hand over my keycard to the POS system and my keys to the club and clap him on the shoulder before making my way to my office. I rarely use it for more than dumping my shit before starting my shift. I don't like being confined to my desk when I can be on the floor with everyone else. Jameson had given me an office for his own reasons, and while I appreciated what he was trying to do by making me feel more important than necessary, I didn't want or need it.

A knock on my door has me grinding my molars, and I ignore it. I know it could be one of two people, and I don't want to talk to either of them. Neither one of them had done anything wrong to even warrant me losing my shit, but I don't want any part of their bullshit right now. I just want out.

"Levi. It's me." Nyx's voice is not a welcome solace like mine is for him when I coddle him and treat him better than I do most people. He really isn't to blame, but he's had something that I haven't, and that cuts even deeper than anything else he could do. It is his mere existence that has me ripping the door open and snapping at him.

"What do you want, Onyx?" I fume while looking down at him as he wrings his fingers until they look ready to pop out of their sockets. Jesus, this fucking kid. I turn away from him and go back to grabbing all the shit I need to finally take home, but his words stop me dead in my tracks.

"I just wanted to talk to you about the other night."

Slowly, I peer over my shoulder, not saying a word, silently waiting for him to continue.

He clears his throat a couple times like the words are

lodged in his dainty little throat. God, I never hated the ground someone walked on more than I do in this moment, and he hasn't done a damn thing. The longer he takes to get his words out, the more time I take ripping him apart, nitpicking and cataloging every bit of him that makes him an inferior being. He is the typical alternative twink who has men fawning over him, although that isn't who he really is in the slightest. He seemed to adopt the style to hide from someone or something. Not that it doesn't suit him because it does, but it seems somewhat unnatural for someone as pretty as him to want to mar his flawless skin with tattoos and piercings that were similar to mine. And while he may be pretty to look at, he is all man in the places that counted. Places that I wasn't. No matter how much money I'd thrown at Dr. Godfrey, there were things we couldn't change and some that I wasn't willing to. She had done amazing work, but in this moment, it felt like we hadn't done a damn thing. Although it made no difference to the people I fucked, but it still felt like a kick in the teeth knowing that he had what Cortland was looking for and Nyx had fucked him. Whether he remembered it or not, he had Cortland in a way that I didn't, and it made me want to ruin his pretty fucking face.

A sniffle makes me turn to face him. His eyes line with unshed tears, glassy and red. His lip trembles when he looks at me, for what I don't know, maybe sympathy, but there's nothing for me to give him right now that could make him feel better.

"Listen, we've all been there. No one is judging you for choices you made." Even as I say those words, meaning every one of them, I can't keep the malice I feel for him out of my cadence. I meant it when I said no one is judging him, but he needs to live with the choices he made.

I just won't absolve him.

"I don't know what happened, and I've been racking my

brain trying to figure it out for the past few days, but I can't grasp onto a single moment. There are flashes here and there, but I can't put any of them together."

"There isn't much I can give you that will help you, Onyx. We picked you up after you called us, I'm assuming before anything happened, but you know who you were with and what you invited into your life when you chose to ignore both Jameson and me after we warned you not to get involved with him." I lean back against my desk with my arms crossed over my chest while he fiddles with the straps of leather cutting into the skin of his waist. I watch as he becomes increasingly more uncomfortable in my presence. A normal person would jump at the opportunity to put someone out of their misery, but I couldn't help loving the way people look when they start to squirm and being the reason for it.

"Did I do something to make you hate me, Levi?" His question worms its way into my heart, nestling itself in the deep recesses of what's left of it. I almost feel bad that he has to ask.

I shrug, looking him dead in the eye, "Not sure what gave you that impression."

"I mean, something has clearly changed between us. You won't even give me the time of day, and you haven't since then, so it had to have been something I did or said that night. What could I have done that was so terrible that the person I was beginning to think was my friend, my first real friend since coming here, would turn their back on me so quickly and without explanation?" There's that backbone I was looking for.

I chuckle to myself, but it makes him scoff. He thinks I'm laughing at his expense and while it is partially true, I am laughing at him, I'm more so laughing at myself for letting this kid get close to me when he should have steered clear of me. I was never the nice guy who had friends, yet here he was. I did start to consider him a friend as well, and maybe that's why all this hurts more than it should, whether he understands why I'm punishing him or not. He had become my friend. But even Jameson doesn't know about my life before Atlanta, and I wasn't about to give Onyx that either.

That part of my life was meant to stay buried. Cortland could stay there too, six feet under with the rest of the bayou.

"We're good, Nyx. If that's all, I really need to finish up here." I wave my hand in front of me where all of my shit is strewn across my desk and chairs in front of it.

Concern eats away at the apprehension as he looks down at my belongings then back up at me like he's trying to do an overcomplicated math problem that has too many letters involved for anyone's comfort.

"Wait, why are you leaving? The night isn't even halfway over yet." He starts babbling about how I can't leave when I notice Cortland leaning against the doorframe, waiting for his turn. "Levi, you can't seriously be leaving. We need you here. Jameson hasn't even finalized everything for the event with PBR."

"I might be able to assist with that." Cortland offers, ever the fucking saint. Of course, he would be involved with the PBR event. To my knowledge, he still rides, and his father supplied the best bulls for the organization, but I don't know what kind of shape he was in now that he was in his thirties or if he was circuit ready. He damn sure looks like it.

"And who are you exactly? Is there a reason you're coming into my office uninvited?" I ask, mainly for show with Nyx still in the room, but I would also like to hear what he has to say.

"You left so abruptly that I didn't get a chance to introduce myself or ask you if you would like to join me for a drink back at my hotel." That shut Nyx up, and myself if I'm being honest.

"Well, you can make an appointment to speak with Jameson, the club owner, and settle everything for the event. If you'll excuse me, I have an obligation that I need to attend to." When the hell did I get so proper?

"I'd be more than happy to walk you out, Levi. That is your name, right?" This fucker.

I roll my eyes as I stuff my last few things in my backpack before shrugging on my leather jacket and picking up my helmet to set it on my desk. I wanted nothing more than to throttle him, but appearances and all that.

"Right. Again, who are you? You seem a little too eager for someone who just got here."

Nyx watches our exchange, his eyes ping-ponging back and forth between us like he isn't sure he should be here but also who the hell he should be looking at.

"Oh, Levi, I've been here for a long time. Longer than I'm sure you want me to admit." He rumbles, trying to goad me.

I scoff as I hike my backpack onto my shoulders and grab my helmet, then I round my desk and stop in front of him on my way out, bringing us chest to chest. I finally allowed myself to really look at him for the first time since seeing him in Alessio's house, really look at him. I tip my head back the slightest bit to get a full view of him underneath the brim of that black cowboy hat I love so much and aim my best grin at him before shutting him down. "Well, if that's the case, I'm sure you have enough patience in you to wait to speak with Jameson rather than me. After all, I'm just the bartender."

I weave through the bodies of clients and dancers, heading for the employee elevator and leaving Cortland and Nyx to entertain themselves. I punch in my code once the doors open and just as the doors nearly seal me inside, a hand shoots between the doors, forcing them to open again. I really can't fucking win. A black cowboy hat comes into view as the doors open, and I curse under my breath when he closes the distance between us. Cortland winks as he backs me into the corner, my helmet knocking against the metal wall behind me.

"Don't you fucking dar—" My protest is cut off by his lips covering mine. His hand comes up to clasp my throat, squeezing just enough to keep me in place as he invades my mouth, his tongue swirling around the barbell pierced through my own before tugging sharply. He pulls the emergency stop button, the ringing ricocheting off the walls and bringing me back to earth. I shove him back, caging him against the wall and my knee connects with his balls. His skull bounces off the metal wall as he throws his head back in pain, making me laugh.

I grab his jaw, forcing him to look at me when I give him one more warning, "Don't fucking touch me, Cortland. I said it once, and I really don't like repeating myself, you do not belong here. I do not want you here, and if you come near me again, I'll kill you."

4
LEVI

'Heartless' Morgan Wallen

What I'd intended to be a couple days turned into a week, a blissful week of uninterrupted peace and quiet. I thought it was going to drive me insane, but after the first two days I found myself sinking into a comfortable routine of being home. I still got myself up and did everything I normally would anyway, but there was no pressure of going into work nearly every night, forcing myself to be on for every person who came into Fallout. Jameson called a few times, but eventually he stopped after the fourth day of no contact.

I wanted to be left alone.

Isolated.

Wind blows through the Spanish moss trees surrounding my house, and it is the most peaceful I've felt in a while. The rustling of the leaves as the trees shake soothe pieces of me that I thought healed a long time ago but were reopened by Cortland's presence. I didn't expect old wounds to fester, weeping until their poison wormed their way through my mind again. If I knew him as well as I once did, he wasn't leaving without a fight, but he'd proven me wrong once before, and I hoped he would this time.

When I ran, I did it with the intention of never being found and I made my peace with the fact I would never lay eyes on the man who taught me how to love again, but he was also the one to teach me what heartbreak felt like. It gutted me to leave him once, but forcing him to leave me this time might break me beyond repair. I made my peace with being alone and he was here to unravel every bit of what I repaired along the way.

I walk back inside and drop my coffee mug in the sink for later. I can't help getting lost in the land in front of me as I stand in front of the sink. I'd made sure the window I created for the kitchen looked out towards the open fields, hoping I'd eventually have something more to look at one day. I didn't let myself get caught up in the fantasy of what I could have if I really wanted to. While I knew I could do it, I wasn't sure that life was meant for me anymore.

Since being home, that fantasy felt closer than I wanted it to be—especially with Cortland wandering around Atlanta unchecked and with Alessio's blessing. I shut it down before it even had a chance to take root.

A chirp pulls me out of my wayward thoughts, and I look down to see Rhydian, one of my Abyssinians, slowly making his way into the kitchen, eyes still half-mast from sleep. He sits at my feet and starts washing one of his delicate paws and then the other before looking up at me, blinking softly.

Rhydian and Spade couldn't be happier, the little mooches. They stuck close as always whenever I was home, but now they had my undivided attention, and I didn't realize until now how much I missed them. They were used to my routine and long hours, which I'm sure I'll be hearing about when I go back to work, but for now I was here until I felt like going back, if I did.

Rhydian purrs as he twines between my legs before throwing himself on the floor and rolling onto his back, showing me his belly, like I would fall for that. It was the oldest trick in the book with cats. They'd bait you in with their cuteness and promises of innocence only to tear your skin off if you touched their soft, squishy bellies. I knew better. Although, I was always tempted with Rhydian. He normally didn't ask for much affection like Spade demanded, but since being home this past week, he was insatiable, and I was more than happy to acquiesce. But I still wasn't touching that murder trap.

After satisfying his needs, I venture back to my bedroom and lean against the doorway, watching my regrets roll around in my sheets for longer than I should. He is gorgeous, I'll give him that. He also scratched an itch I couldn't reach on my own, but now it was time for him to go. Yeah, I don't really regret him—I just don't want to deal with this shit in the morning, when you have to sit back and watch someone get themselves together in the daylight and the frenzied high feeling of their skin against yours evaporated the night before.

"Thiago, get out." I announce a little louder than necessary and rip the sheets off him. He scrambles a little too much for my liking, but at least he's awake.

"Jesus, Reigns, some fucking decency." He gripes as he sits up, his hard cock on display and making my mouth water.

Taking it a step further, I toss his clothes at him for good measure. "You weren't concerned about decency last night, in fact what we did was anything but, and now it's time for you to go."

"How many times are we gonna do this before you let me

—" He quiets when I tilt my head, arching my brow in his direction. Thiago knew the score, and this is why I didn't do repeats—they got too comfortable.

"We're not doing anything other than this." I gesture around the room like we're in containment, like these four walls are the only place that would have us together in any capacity, although that isn't true. We see each other too often at meets, but what we do here is never going to make it out in the real world. We call each other when we have an itch, and that's it.

He scoffs, rolling his eyes like an indignant child when they don't get their way. The only thing missing is him sucking his teeth and storming off to his room.

"Do as you're told. This conversation isn't going anywhere worthy of our time, and we both know it." I slam the door, leaving him alone to get that through his thick skull.

I settle into my favorite chair in the corner of my living room, away from all the furniture that could give someone an opportunity to sit next to me, and wait for him to walk out. Spade joins me, perching himself at my side and stretching his front legs along my thigh while Rhydian curls up at my feet like they're waiting for the same thing, for us to be alone again. It doesn't take Thiago long before he emerges from my bedroom fully clothed and looking like he could spit nails. He's always been a surly fuck, but this seems like overkill.

He stalks over to me and before I have time to get out of reach, he grabs me by the throat and yanks me from my chair, making Spade hiss at him before slinking off to the bedroom. I gain my balance enough to get my feet under me and stare up at him, waiting for him to get this little temper tantrum over with.

"You have a mouth on you that's gonna get you into a world of hurtin' one of these days." He rumbles before slanting his lips over mine and invading my mouth. His tongue traces every soft tissue he can reach as if he's trying to imprint himself, leaving a permanent reminder that he'd been there. As much as I fight it, I groan, allowing myself to fall into his body for just a moment. A single moment of comfort. His spicy scent mixed with the smell of us still on his skin is dizzying, intoxicating as it infiltrates my senses and subdues me to his advances. The warmth of his skin seeping into the chilled, aching joints of each of my fingers that only gives the more I pull his hard body into mine.

Thiago's words echo in my mind as he takes me apart, but it isn't his voice whispering them in my ear. He wasn't the first person to tell me that and surely wouldn't be the last.

I do my level best to detach myself from him, to say something that would push him away from me even further. The hold he has on me is more than I can bear. At the crux of it all, he's right. About too many things because he's seen more than I've let anyone else see. While Jameson and his family took me in with no questions, Thiago has always been the closest to me in a way that Cortland had been. I can discount it in my mind and dress it up as much as I want, but a pig in makeup will always be a pig. Just like Thiago would always be the "what if" and never the end all. He could try to push for more than I could give him, but it would never end in us having the happily ever after he was so intent on us having. He deserved more than the scraps left of me that still belonged to another man who would never claim them.

"Thi, we're never going to be what you need us to be." I murmur against his lips between bone melting kisses. I feel my soul shattering just a little more each time he pulls away before sinking back into me, sipping each breath from my lips until there's little left for me to do but submit to his will.

"Keep pushing every person away, and you'll end up alone, Levi." He promises as he places kisses along my cheek bone while his hands tighten at the nape of my neck until I give into the pressure and let my head fall back, giving into him.

An abrupt banging on my front door forces Thiago to pull back and look down at me like I should know who it is, and I do. I knew he'd find me eventually. It was simply a matter of when.

"Time's up, Woods." I force a smile that even I know isn't the least bit convincing to either one of us. I take one last look at his beautiful face. Even though I'd done a number on him, he was still one of the most beautiful men I'd ever seen. Thankfully the good doctor patched him up, and the scar should be no more than a faint silvery reminder of the mistakes we made. I never apologized to anyone, but I felt a small amount of guilt for letting my emotions get the better of me when Thiago had lost his shit on me at the meet. Although Dr. Godfrey wasn't too happy with me for what I'd done to him, Thiago hadn't held it against me.

The banging starts again and stops, and Thiago stares at the door for a moment then presses a softer kiss against my temple just as I realize why it stopped. Cortland appears in the doorway of the kitchen, watching as Thiago slowly pulls away from me, his hands lingering on my waist longer than necessary. Thi stiffens against me when it registers that someone is watching us and we are no longer alone.

His eyes snap to mine, anger filling his pale green irises, "Are you fucking serious? Him?"

"You should go. We'll see each other around, yeah?" I take a step back, gnawing at my lip and avoiding his eyes. I'd never cared about the effects my actions had on anyone, but this time felt like I was cutting off a limb. We would never be the same after this.

5

CORTLAND

'Out Of Oklahoma' Lainey Wilson

I'd waited as long as I could before tracking Levi down. He'd wanted space, and I'd given it to him. He wanted to be left alone, and I understood. I knew when I could push his boundaries, and this was not one of those times, but I'd given him enough to let him resume his normal life for a week before calling in a favor to find his address—an active address.

Levi's somehow managed to acquire quite a few properties over the years, but the one I wanted was where he went to hide. Imagine my surprise when it was a little slice of heaven hidden in Savannah with acres and acres of open land unblemished by the outside world. It had been someone's ranch at some point, unless Levi had built this and was taking care of the upkeep by himself. I realized just how secretive he'd become since he left Louisiana, especially since no one had any idea that he'd done all of this, let alone knew he owned it. Well, except Alessio, but he wasn't out here spilling people secrets, and when I'd asked him to give me something, he hesitated. In his own way, that was how Alessio showed he loved someone.

As I drove up the winding paved driveway to the main house sitting under Spanish moss trees, tears pricked my eyes, emotions clogging my throat at the sight. It was everything Levi had said he always wanted. A house hidden beneath the trees that he loved, a small southern oasis. There was no other way to describe it. I knew Levi wanted nothing more than to get away from the life he'd had before hiding out in Georgia, and I could see and feel it in the way he spoke and how he avoided personal questions, but some things never die, no matter how deep you bury them.

His bike sat out front with a truck that had him written all over it, a stark white GMC Sierra 2500, lifted with just a smidge of chrome that could never be considered gaudy. Both sat in front of black modern rancher style home with a wraparound porch complete with rocking chairs just like his momma loved. Of course, Levi had infused his style into the exterior of the home in a way his momma would have loved, even if it wasn't a classic ranch, but he'd loved his momma more than words could ever express, and it showed in the way he built this. It was like he'd done it with her in mind, like she would eventually see it. I didn't know if that would ever happen, but damn if I didn't want to move heaven and earth to make it so.

It was a bittersweet sight.

The only thing sticking out like a sore thumb was the black Dodge Charger parked next to Levi's bike, the same one I'd seen at that car meet. It felt like I'd been stuck by a cattle prod.

That bittersweet feeling became overwhelmed by a sickening rage as I jerked my truck into park in front of the house and tried to get a handle on it before getting out and bounding up the few stairs leading to the porch. I waited for a moment, counting to ten again, even though it did nothing to settle my erratic heartbeat, then started darkening the front door. I could make out the two of them standing together in the living room a little too close. When neither of them got any sense of urgency, I banged on the door again before stopping abruptly and walking around the side of the house. If it was anything like Mrs. Sorensen's, Levi would have added a door that led directly into the kitchen. And if he was really like his momma, he never fucking locked that door if he was home.

I sent up a silent prayer hoping I was right when I reached for the handle and pressed down on the latch. A sigh of relief escaped me when the door opened with an ease I didn't feel. I could hear Levi murmuring something to that kid, softer than I thought he was capable of.

Somehow, I had enough restraint to keep myself from interrupting them as they embraced each other far too long for them to have been the enemies they appeared to be on the black top. And I sure as hell wouldn't be standing that close to a man who deserved to be sliced from stem to stern for something that came out of his mouth less than two weeks ago. I'd missed something, or Alessio had, because it looked like they were lovers. There was a gentleness to the way Woods–yeah, I remember his name–handled Levi that I wouldn't have expected from someone who spouted so much hate for the man in his arms.

It didn't take long for Levi to notice me. We'd always been attuned to each other, knowing when the other was near without having to even look. It was a feeling so palpable, so strong, and completely impossible to ignore. We joked about it especially when people began noticing we'd become close and spent probably too much time together, but it wasn't like we were told not to. It was encouraged regardless of Levi being less than legal at seventeen years old while I had been twenty-nine at the time. It was sickening. The feelings I had developed for Levi during those last few years before he'd left were no one's fault but my own. Looking back at it now, I knew it was wrong, whether he had pursued me or not, encouraged by our parents or not. I should have cut ties with him before it went too far, but I could never bring myself to do it, and that fact still haunted me even now as I stood in his kitchen.

Hell, both of our fathers seemed more than thrilled by the idea that we could join the families and form some fucked up dynasty. Of course, until Levi chose to come out. And while I was prouder of him than I'd ever been, I was terrified of what they might do to him.

It took every drop of willpower I had left to stay rooted in place when Woods pressed a delicate, barely-there kiss to Levi's temple, but knowing I'd have Levi to myself with no escape made it bearable. I wasn't a man who thrived on the idea of stripping someone of their free will, and I never had been until Levi. The thought of bending him to my will and forcing him into submission until the only thing concerning him was me quickly became more intoxicating than anything I'd ever experienced.

Woods whipped his head in my direction, confusion and hurt etching his features. His pale green irises ignited as the pieces started falling into place and his hands tighten on Levi's waist like that would change the outcome.

"Are you fucking serious? Him?" He barked in Levi's face. Neither of us tried to deny it. I certainly had no intention of letting either of them believe I wasn't getting what I came here for. I told Levi a week ago, and I'd meant it.

Levi took a step back and another, shaking his head in disbelief, but his words came out crystal clear, "You should go. We'll see each other around, yeah?"

I watch as the cockiness drains from Woods, and his body

deflates in defeat. Poor kid didn't stand a chance. While it was still a gamble that I'd leave here today having what I wanted, I knew all too well what it felt like to lose Levi. The ache never went away. It festered, rearing its ugly head on nights I was too weak to shove the brimming emotions back down until I had no choice but to drown in them. The same nights I wanted nothing more than to bury myself in him, whether I'd had a good night on the circuit, or I was fighting against an immovable obstacle like Marcus, I'd find myself seconds away from jumping into my truck and booking it to Georgia even if it was only to breathe the same air.

"I hope he's worth it, Vi." Woods forces out, cutting another scathing look in my direction but grabs his keys and jacket from the back of the couch. On his way out the door he takes a moment to look at me like he's seeing me for the first time."He survived this long without you, you know. Don't make him learn how to do it again if you aren't willing to give him everything."

I nod. Although I hate him for being a bigger part of Levi's life than I had thought he was, I couldn't argue with him. I knew I needed to be more than sure about the decision I was about to make. It wasn't just Levi who I'd be uprooting. I had to think about Diana and Elliott, and the business, while keeping them all safe.

Levi and I both leave his words hanging between us like a guillotine waiting for a single false move as we watch Woods leave. I see why Levi would have wanted him. He's gorgeous, even I could see that. Deep tanned skin, tattoos sprawling down his muscled arms to the backs of his hands and tight cropped black curls with green eyes. Throw in the fact that he was a street racer or whatever it was they did, and he was the typical bad boy who had men and women drooling over him. And I'd bet that was what captivated Levi in the first place.

He never could say no to what wasn't good for him. The similarities were there; we just had different vices.

"I'm only going to ask you this one more time, and honestly if you can't answer the question, you need to stay away from me," Levi threatens as he remains on the other side of the room, further from me than I really want. His head lulls to the side as he takes me apart with calculating eyes before meeting mine before his sigh turns into a bitter, hollow laugh. "Why are you here, Cortland?"

I knew the answer he wanted, and I wanted to give it to him because I was here for him, but it wasn't the whole truth. I made myself available to Jameson for the PBR event to get closer to Levi, but it wasn't necessary. Neil, the PR manager for PBR, was already working with Jameson, and I didn't give a damn about it. In the same vein, I knew if I didn't give Levi an answer, he would make good on doing everything in his power to keep me away. So, I settled on a half-truth I hoped wouldn't send him running.

I slowly took a step closer to him and kept my movements controlled, even though I itched to plaster his body against mine again, just to revel in the fact that I could. But instead, I kept my hands to myself and gave him something else. "I'm here for you, Levi. You were always the goal."

Levi doesn't say anything, he just continues to stare at me, but this time it doesn't seem like he's seeing anything. I wait for some sign that he heard me, but he remains unfocused in a trance-like state, looking right through me. I think for a moment I might have broken him before a soft smile tugs at the corners of his mouth that he stops in its tracks.

"If you're lying, I'll kill you."

HE HAS CATS. I'm not sure why it shocks me, but it does. And they couldn't just be normal cats either—no, they were big fuckers, burnt orange with brown markings unlike any I'd seen before. I don't remember a time that Levi ever said anything about wanting or even liking the nefarious things. I didn't hate them. They had a job and did it well on my ranch, but I didn't particularly go out of my way to be around them. Not like I did with Gritty, Duchess, and Strike, my border collies, and Tracer, our livestock guardian, although he wasn't ever in the house like the girls were. They all had jobs, but the cats kept to themselves, and I preferred to keep it that way.

"He's not going to attack you, but if you keep staring at him like that, he might get offended," Levi says as he brushes past me to make his way over to his chair before curling up in it with said cat.

I grumble to myself as I take off my cowboy hat and go to hang it up but think better of it, needing to keep my hands occupied. While Levi watches my every move, I take in the home he built, noting each novelty adorning the walls. Some pieces he'd acquired over the years are vintage western art or décor I hoped I would find while others were newer and feel like a glimpse into his life without me. It feels as though I am taking in physical manifestations of two completely different people who reconcile into one cohesive being that is Levi. When my eyes settle on a framed photo, my heart almost gives out.

"I was wondering how long it would take you to find that." His breath tickles the back of my neck, making the hairs stand on end. I hadn't heard him get up, but his front is nearly touching my back, only a few inches keeping us apart from a salvation both of us yearn for.

Distracted by his proximity, I forget what I'd even been looking at until he reaches around me to pick up the photo. He's careful not to let our fingers touch when he hands it to me, but this time he doesn't take a step back. He stays right next to me, close enough that each time he inhales, his chest brushes against my arm. When I finally pull my eyes away from him, I feel my heart leap into my throat as I look at the photo again, taking in every piece of him atop his stunning mare in all his show wear. His hair was longer then too and had been curled, I'm sure, within an inch of its life before being pulled into a ponytail so he could easily wear his signature black and emerald rhinestone studded cowboy hat that matched the silk button up show shirt. My favorite piece of the attire was the black suede fringed chaps he'd always worn, and by God, they fit him like a fucking glove.

The photo was one I'd taken of him during one of his last shows with his mare, Hera, who'd been his champion in the reining show pen. He hated reining, but he was made for it. She went on to be a part of his breeding program when he retired her, and she was my son's favorite. She's also the mare who is Ares' dam. She's every bit the typical mare who people chalked up as temperamental, mean, and could be downright nasty when she was in foal, but she was an amazing mover, and when she loved you, she'd do anything you'd ask her to. She always made you work for her affection, but once you had it, that was it for her. Hera ended up being Levi's only reining horse and his only true black mare, much to his dismay, with a striking bald face, and begrudgingly she had been his heart horse. I knew it gutted him to leave behind his horses, but he had no choice.

As we both look at the photo together, he seems to shrink inside himself the longer we do. I take a risk and tip his chin up so I can see what is happening behind those eyes, and all I can see is a war he'd been fighting since I laid eyes on him. While my thumb caresses the fine bones of his trembling jaw, I press a kiss to his forehead and whisper words I hope would bring him peace. "She's happy, you know. Still a rank bitch, but she's happy."

The frame shakes in his hand as he puts it back where it belongs, but that is the only indication he's heard me. He doesn't run, but he doesn't say anything when he takes a small step back to create space between us again, and I don't force him to come back to me—this time I won't, but if he starts running, it's out of my hands.

Levi goes into the kitchen and comes back with a beer and a tumbler of whiskey he hands to me on his way over to his chair. That fucking chair is going to be the death of me, but I guess that's the point. He wants to keep his distance not just from me but anyone he invites into his space.

I watch as he shoves the lime wedge into his *Corona* with his thumb and then without thinking wraps his lips around the digit to suck the remnants of sticky juice from his skin. The act is innocent, but my cock stirs to life anyway, pressing painfully against the metal teeth of my zipper. I curse under my breath and take a deep breath when he raises the bottle to his lips and watch his throat work as he drinks.

Taking a healthy gulp of my own drink, I try to rein in my impulses. Ones that would fuck everything up before we were even able to get our cards on the table, although I'd been avoiding that since I got here. We needed to get it out the way, and my dick was not a part of this equation. At least, not right now.

"You havin' an issue keepin' your head on straight over there, cowboy?" Levi asks, but he knows the answer. I track his eyes as they dilate when they land on my denim-covered crotch. A wolfish, almost sinister grin graces his handsome face the longer I stay quiet.

"You tell me, baby?" I taunt and that grin starts to slip the moment I adjust myself and spread my thighs to give myself some breathing room.

I lean all the way back and stretch one of my arms across the back of the couch while I rest my right hand on my thigh, tapping my fingers against the muscle, challenging Levi while keeping my gaze on him the entire time. He takes another swig off his beer before setting it aside. I wait for him to decide, whether he comes over to me or not is entirely up to him, but if he does, I'm not letting him go until he accepts he's mine.

I wasn't normally a selfish man, but I was possessive in my own way, but in this I knew it was absolute. I'd let him go once to keep him breathing, but now there was nothing that could possibly keep me from him if he gave in. And I will tell him as much. I want no room for miscommunication, no room for misinterpretation. He needs to know what he is getting himself into.

"Be sure, Levi." I demand as he unfolds himself to stand, long legs covered in tattoos down to his feet eat up the distance at an agonizing pace. I need him to be decisive. The closer he gets to me, the harder my heart batters against my ribcage, until his knees brush mine.

I look up at the man standing in front of me, and I have never been more unsure of what he might do. I know what I want him to do, but he is impossible for me to read, and that's a foreign feeling between us.

As I continue taking in the sight of him, he's never been more beautiful. It was the lean, hardened muscle he'd built to hide the delicate boning he was born with. He is no longer drowning in oversized clothing, the sharpness of his features no longer obscured by a veil of thick black curls, the fine bones of his hands now disguised by intricate black ink covering the back of his hands and each finger. He is no longer the gangly, knobby-kneed kid who shot up to six feet and was playing hell to catch up. He's every bit who he was meant to be. But when he's like this, soft and pliant—

willing and no longer full of piss and vinegar—he is breathtaking.

The moment he lowers himself to his knees in front of me, laying his head in my lap and nuzzling my aching cock with his nose before settling against me, a familiar burning assaulted the bridge of my nose, the pain that flared in my chest and hadn't stopped since the day he ran away finally began to soothe and uncoil itself.

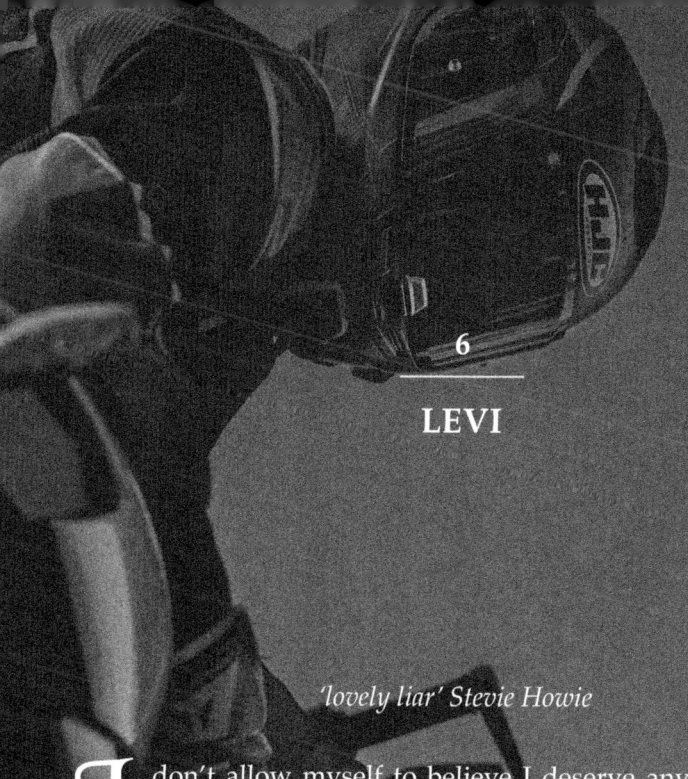

6

LEVI

'lovely liar' Stevie Howie

I don't allow myself to believe I deserve anything good that's ripe for the taking, but Cortland offers himself up to me time and time again. And for him, I am a weak man.

He hasn't shied away from me when I've given him numerous reasons he should run like hell. No, he keeps digging his heels in and fighting like hell the same way he did when he was riding one of the rankest bulls on the circuit, holding on for eight seconds.

The familiar roughness of his jeans presses against my cheek when I burrow my head in his lap, making myself at home in his warmth. I nuzzle further into him, seeking as much of him as I can possibly reach from this angle. His cock twitches as I nudge him gently and inhale his scent. Cortland always smelled of my favorite things that became synonymous with him each time I caught their scent—black cherries, chocolate and tobacco smoke—but his sweat and musk that were unique to him were beyond comparison. It was dark and rich, decadent almost, and I was a glutton. I would never be satisfied with moderation if Cortland was on the menu.

Cortland's hand settles on the back of my head, applying the slightest pressure until I give in, burying my face in his crotch. His breathing becomes erratic when I wrap my lips around his dick, mouthing the hard length through his jeans until his head falls back against the couch. I watch in fascination as his mouth falls open when I press my tongue to the head of his cock, tasting the wet spot he'd already created. The moment his flavor burst over my taste buds, I knew I would never get enough of him. A pathetic whine escapes me as I seek out more before I can stop it and I freeze, shame halting my movements, but Cortland stops me from pulling away before I even start, forcing me to take what is given.

I'd never felt shame with any of my previous partners because we either never saw each other again, or we understood each other's desires, but with Cortland, I worry I will embarrass him or myself by the things I want and he never had a chance to experience. It makes me wonder if we aren't compatible, and we are only holding onto old wounds and stolen moments.

I don't have time to question it before Cortland makes the decision for me. Instead of allowing me to sink further into my head, he pulls me into his lap and grabs my jaw, bringing me so close I can feel each of his next words on my lips.

"Stop hiding from me, baby. I'm sure you could smell what I like doing to boys on Nyx's skin." Rage spikes in my veins, but the pain radiating in my chest is so much worse. It may as well have been a physical blow to my solar plexus hearing Nyx's name when Cortland has me like this, in his lap and practically begging for his touch. I sure as hell don't want or need the reminder, but I do my best not to let it show.

Looking down at his smug face, I give him a smile he'd seen more times than he'd like before making him a promise I hope he never makes me follow through with. "If you mention another man when you have me in your lap again, we're done. Got it?"

His brows furrow slightly. "You have nothing to worry about."

Even as he says the words I want to hear, it doesn't change how I already feel, whether it's his fault or not. In some ways, he wasn't to blame for the insecurities I had unknowingly fostered over the years, but they were there, and it seemed like they only made themselves known when he was involved.

"If you say so," I shrug, but the tightness in my chest isn't going away. "Who you fuck is your business, not mine."

He rears back as if I'd slapped him, but rather than letting me go, he pulls me impossibly close and whispers in my ear, "When did I ever give you the idea that I'd be fucking anyone other than you, Levi?"

I tremble against him, a deep tremor going through my body at his words. I shake my head, refusing to answer him, and he lets out a low growl, but rather than letting me go, he does something I never thought he would.

As his tongue meets the heated flesh of my neck, I can't help the moan filling the silence for me, but he doesn't stop until he licks up the side of my face like a fucking freak, and arousal seeps into my briefs. It had taken every bit of restraint I had to not immediately wrap myself around Cortland and use his body like a blowup sex doll when he'd pulled me into his lap, but now he'd given me an invitation.

I drop down into his lap like he's my favorite saddle, not shy for a second about giving him all of my weight. I'm not exactly the skin and bones mess I used to be when I was under careful watch of numerous trainers and my father. I'd packed on as much muscle as my body would allow, but it took time to stop hearing their voices taunting me. They'd creep back in if I let them, causing more damage every time now that I wasn't hiding behind a life meant for someone else.

Cortland's groan pulls me back to the present when he lifts his hip, seeking me out, and I can't resist grinding my cock against his with a roll of my hips. The air conditioning kicks on, sending a chill down my spine and causing goosebumps to break out across my overheated flesh as the frigid air bursts the cozy bubble around us. Another whimper forces its way up my throat while I shiver in his lap and every little movement hits my core, increasing my need for his hands on me by tenfold.

A dark chuckle meets my ears as his arms snake around my waist, preventing me from bucking into him. He doesn't hesitate to take advantage of our position and flips us, so I'm seated and he's now between my legs, forcing them apart with his bulk.

It's been a long time since I let anyone take the reins, controlling the pace, but more importantly, me. With Cortland, it comes naturally. Outside of the handful of times we'd fooled around, I didn't defer to him, and I wouldn't now, but I needed him to take control. He seemed to always know it and easily stepped into the role even when I didn't know what it meant, and we never had any formal conversation or means to explore what we could be. Every stolen moment was rushed and at the time felt more than worth the risk. But here I am, sinking into it with him without prompting, without any regard for my safety. It's dangerous and downright reckless.

I could hear my mentor's, Isaiah, voice like he was standing in the room with us, a look of disappointment evident in his eyes before admonishing my behavior with a single tsk and the use of my name like he hadn't spent years training me in both roles, dominant and submissive, and the implications of not playing safe. He's one of the very few people who I hated knowing I'd disappointed him in some way. Not that he would show it—it was something I just felt, charging the air around us when we were in a scene. He always moved on quickly, never harping on anything, but it was hard to keep focus when I knew I had fucked up.

One would think I learned something from the man in the many years I'd been burrowing myself under his wing, but clearly, I hadn't if this is the situation with Cortland I let myself fall into.

With Cortland firmly between my legs, making himself right at home, I watch and wait for him to make the next move. Thankfully, I don't have to wait long, but where his hands are headed brought back the same hesitancy I'd felt a few moments ago. He pulls back slightly, his hands leaving a scorching trail along my skin where my shirt has ridden up my back and abdomen before settling on my shorts. His fingers tease at the waistband as though he's asking for permission, which feels strange. Cortland is not a man who uses caution for much—he's a bully like that—but whatever he saw when he looked at me made him pause, waiting for some indication that I'm ready.

It isn't as though he isn't aware. He knows. I'd let him touch me before, but that was before I'd been on testosterone. Back then I wasn't any different, and I knew his track record. He fucked anything with a pulse to keep up appearances, especially with his father, so I wasn't nervous and didn't feel like I had a reason to be when I hadn't started transitioning. I had been like any other cis woman he'd fucked, but now as a fully transitioned man who wanted nothing to do with bottom surgery, I felt unsure. So many questions and doubts swirl in my mind until a pit of anxiety forms in my chest, and I feel like I'm running out of oxygen.

He starts pulling away, and I immediately feel the loss of his hands on me deep in my bones, but he doesn't deprive me like I feared. He takes my face in his hands and looks me in the eye for what feels like a lifetime while his thumbs slowly trace over my cheekbones, and I give in to him trying to give me comfort until I feel like I can breathe again.

He repeats the same words he'd said to me before, and the tightness uncoils in my chest, and the rest of my body relaxes as he holds my gaze hostage, refusing to waiver. "Levi, you have nothing to worry about. Never with me." When I don't respond, he shakes me a little and clings to me. "Do you hear me?" The biting edge to his voice and fierceness in his eyes paired with the almost brutal grip he has on me is almost too much to handle.

He wants me to answer but seeing him look like this when I am the object of his attention makes it hard to form words. It seems impossible. He's here in my home, pressed between my legs and waiting for me to let him take me apart piece by piece. I keep waiting for someone to pinch me or to jerk awake in a cold sweat, gasping for air, but it wasn't happening. The other shoe was supposed to drop, and it wasn't. No matter how many times I blink, he remains in place.

When I finally seem to be able to pry my tongue from the roof of my mouth to form some kind of response, it comes out in a garbled, embarrassing mess, "Cortland, I...–yes, fuck."

Like the shithead he is, he just smiles, crooked as ever with the devil gleaming in his eyes like he won some prize. And maybe he did. Fucking Satan in a Sunday hat if you ask me.

Rather than him stripping me bare in the blink of an eye

like I expect him to, he slowly inches his hands inside the legs of my shorts until he has two handfuls of my ass and squeezes roughly. He jerks me forward a bit until my ass is nearly hanging off the couch cushion. I eye him for a moment, forcing myself to focus on anything other than the fact he's looking at me like that. Like his world begins and ends with me when it couldn't be further from the truth. He'd gotten it all from what I understood of him since he unknowingly waltzed back in my life, and there was nothing I had that would make a bit of difference to his life.

A slap blisters across my outer thigh, taking me by surprise, and I can't help but gape at him for a moment before shooting up off the couch and barking in his face, "What the hell, Cort?"

Not a second later my knees crack against the hardwood floor, and my head's being wrench back so far it makes me gag and cough from the force, his fingers tangling in the mess of curls at the nape of my neck. Irritation and disappointment rolling off him in tidal waves kept me from complaining, then he opened that sinful mouth of his again. "When did I ever give you the impression that I would keep lettin' you run that fuckin' mouth of yours, peach?"

I don't know what shocks me more, the nickname he's not called me since I came out to him or the smooth swiftness each time he corrected a behavior he didn't like. Cortland was quick to make it known when he was dissatisfied by something, but being on the receiving end of his strength when he was less than pleased by me lashing out was something else entirely, and it made me want to push him far enough to see him snap. I wanted to be on the other end of his leash when he forced me into submission, to heel for him and obey. I just had no intention of making it easy, and we both knew it.

I can't help the maniacal laugh spilling out of me as he

looks down at me with such a severeness to him that it reminds me of the way someone would look at their friend when they're making a situation worse. It's a look I'm definitely used to, but on him it seems worse. My laughter ricochets around my living room, seeking refuge in anything willing to absorb the ear-splitting sound I can't reign in despite myself.

"You look like you're enjoying yourself there. Are you done?" He says, his voice filled with amusement as he stares down at me where he still holds me in place, refusing to give even the barest amount of slack. My scalp starts burning under his fingertips, and my knees scream for relief that's never coming if I keep going on like this, but the sensation skittering along my skin and the low humming in my brain make it hard to see that as a problem when it feels like I might burst into flames at any moment.

"You tell me, cowboy. Am I done?" I taunt, despite knowing he might put me on my ass. I could see the war and indecision behind his eyes the more I pushed him, but it's the only indication he gives. He doesn't ruffle easily and never has, but as much as he wants to break me—I want to see him shattered. I want him to be unrecognizable to anyone but me.

As Cortland stands over me fully clothed, not a hair out of place, while I'm on my knees for him panting like a bitch in heat, a sense of calm washes over me. And fuck if I don't want to be bred by this man.

"Since you want to be a bratty little shit and won't let me make this better than what you got last time, I'll give you a choice, very simple. We wouldn't want anyone to think I treat you less than gentlemanly now, would we?" He says, his eyes twinkling with the promises of pain. He pops on the cheek for good measure, making my nostrils flare before continuing. "We can keep this nice and sweet like you should've gotten, or we can do this my way, and you take what I give you without the attitude. Your choice."

I knew my answer before he finished, but he wanted certainty, assurance. "I'll take what you give me."

"Get up." The demand startles me slightly, making me hesitate long enough that he yanks me to my feet and my eye line is filled by his full dusky pink lips. There's an asymmetry to them that I've always loved, his lower lip a smidge larger than his top lip and the neatly trimmed dark blonde beard that he'd had for as long as I could remember making them look even fuller, decadent like chocolate cake—so rich and sweet it'll rot your teeth if you're not careful.

With Cortland, I know I need to use caution for once in my life. He's a walking heartbreak waiting like a snake in the grass, striking when you least expect it then slithering away like it never happened.

He pulls me down the hallway until we stop in front of my bedroom and the sight before me makes me nauseous. Sheets still rumpled and very obviously stained by a unique cocktail of mine and Thiago's sweat and cum, my clothes from the night before strewn across the floor and boots thrown in opposite directions—all of it really painting a masterpiece of what happened when we got back after being at a meet last night. There is no hiding it, although Cortland I'm sure had already drawn whatever conclusions from seeing us together when he showed up unannounced, and he wouldn't be wrong.

"You aren't getting out of this. I would still fuck you if his cum was still dripping from your cunt, peach." His lips brush against my ear, making me shiver as he makes it crystal clear he doesn't give a fuck that he's about to fuck me in the same bed with the same sheets still on the damn thing.

"I bet you would, you dirty old bastard." I huff under my

breath, rolling my eyes like it doesn't get my dick hard thinking about him using someone else's nut as lube. I almost wish I hadn't already showered just to see how far I could push him.

Cortland doesn't miss it though. "You wanna repeat that, boy?" He asks as he pushes me through the doorway and walks past me with too much ease in his gait. My jaw tics as I stare down at the filthy black satin sheets in front of me, and for a split second, I regret what I did the night before.

"I didn't realize you'd started losing your hearing already in your old age. Should I invest in some hearing aids for you?" I quip, but I keep my back to him to prevent him seeing I might be crumbling whether I want to or not.

There's a beat of silence followed by a noise I can't decipher, and I lift my gaze to look over my shoulder to find him unbuckling his belt and letting the tail of it, along with the platinum buckle he'd gotten from his first championship, dangles from the belt loops of his beat-to-hell blue jeans. He's a fucking sight. His hand moves to the button of his jeans, and I track the movement like a starved predator waiting for the opportune moment to pounce, sinking my teeth into his flesh and consuming him until there's no trace of him left behind.

Cortland studies me for a moment, his gaze trained on my throat before meeting my eyes, "What'd I say about the attitude, huh? When are you gonna learn that that mouth of yours is just gonna land you in a world of hurt with me?"

I slowly turn to face him before speaking slowly so he'll get the picture, "I don't know, Cortland. When are you going to give me what I asked for and stop pussyfooting around?" The false bravado while I'm shaking in my boots is only going to get me so far, but I can't stop myself from plucking his nerves.

"So intent on making this something cheap when I made

it clear we would be anything but. Why? Is it because that's all you're good for now?" He muses with a tinge of unmistakable judgement lacing its way through his voice. Not taking a step forward but also not backing away to leave, he leans against the chest of drawers lining the wall facing the bed and crosses his arms over his wide chest.

When I don't jump at the chance to defend myself, one dark blonde brow arches up as if to prompt me. Any other time with any other person, I would have told them to get out because it was no one's business what made me like this—cold and heartless. But the reason was standing right in front of me. *Willingly.* I'd never wanted to cut a man off at the knees more than I did in this moment, and all my logic seems to have clocked out for the day. I almost feel bad for him, and I haven't even opened my mouth yet.

Momma always said, "Don't stoop to their level, baby. Raise above." I could take her advice. I could let him get on with it. I could let him make assumptions. I also could ignore it if I were a better person—I'm not.

Before I open my mouth, something dies inside of me. A small piece of me—miniscule. A piece I'll never get back, but I've already lost so much along the way that I don't have it in me to fight for what's left of me anymore. Cortland had seen me in my wreckage and is seeing me in my rebirth, but it feels like he's still looking for the same little girl who doted on him, who thought he'd hung the moon and stars for her. His little show pony. But I was never that little girl, and never would be.

We could sit here and split hairs about intention, whether he meant it or not, but I'd already accepted too much for too long.

"I didn't take you for stupid," I say, my voice dropping an octave. My change in cadence momentarily stuns him and the color drains from his face, and sick satisfaction warms my chest. He remains silent as I take a step in his direction. "Did you run out of steam already? Performance anxiety? That's pathetic. I thought you had all the answers, Thierry, or was that just when you assumed I would automatically obey?"

It isn't often someone worms their way under my skin and provokes me, but I let my guard down a little bit, and this is what I get.

"Nothing to say. Figures. You never could stand up for yourself, or me for that matter. Jesus, Cortland, if your daddy could see you now, he'd be disappointed, wouldn't he? Tell me, does he know that his son likes to leave his wife at home to go fuck men? Does the great Marcus Thierry know his son is an adulterous sodomite?" The mention of his father makes his nostrils flare, and a familiar fire ignites in his eyes that I was sure had been snuffed out by years of abuse at the hands of his father, but it's not a deterrent for me. If anything, it's the accelerant I'm craving. Even as I continue berating him with insults and questions while inching forward, until I'm standing chest to chest with him, his chest heaving like he ran a marathon…he refuses to break.

The thrum of blood coursing beneath my heated flesh doesn't even begin to temper itself as Cortland stares down at me. It's a heady feeling, so addictive and sweet I can almost taste it, like getting your first slide on a colt after weeks of building their confidence. The thought brings my brain to screeching halt as soon as it forms, shocking me for a moment. I hadn't thought about my horses, let alone what it was like training and riding them, in years—at least that's what I'm going to keep telling myself. Deep down, they'd always be my first love, but they deserved better than someone like me. Just like everyone else around me deserving better than getting saddled with me.

A pin could drop, and the world would hear it from inside my bedroom. Cortland hadn't moved an inch, hadn't uttered a single word nor had he done anything other than stare into my soul—a soul he's corroded until it won't allow anyone else in to fill the hole he left behind.

We stand so close to one another I can taste the leashed anger simmering beneath his skin, skin flushed by emotion I provoked. This close, I can see the striations of honey set ablaze in his whiskey irises. They are mesmerizing. Most people always talk about how blue or green eyes were the best, most beautiful enrapturing thing, but I'd always preferred drowning in whiskey.

The pulse of his carotid jumps as his jaw tenses, and his body starts vibrating against mine, his hands now fisted at his sides like it would stop him striking me in anger, but I want him to. Something to show me he was still in there, that I hadn't broken him.

So, I wait, listening to the hum of electricity working its way through the house. I don't dare move. I don't take my eyes off him—I couldn't even if I wanted to. I was incapable of looking away from him, even if it would have saved me from the years of torment that he'd seen me endure firsthand. I damn sure wasn't looking away now especially when I finally have him right where I want him.

Watching him teeter on the edge of a blade I'm offering him is a rush like no other. If I were smarter, I wouldn't be standing here, but now that I'd had a hit, I'm not sure I can handle hitting rock bottom.

"As entertaining as that was, I hope you got it out of your system." Cortland says, his voice now rough and gravelly like his vocal cords were put through a blender.

Reluctantly, I lift my gaze from his lips to meet his eyes and pout for a moment before smiling. "No, it never will be, so get used to it. Your judgment isn't warranted here, and you have no room to pass any kind of judgment on my life, nor what I've done to repair the damage inflicted. As I recall, you weren't and have never been one to exercise a shred of loyalty to any partner you've had, and now you have a wife, Cortland, so what does that say about you?"

We hadn't discussed it, and truthfully, I didn't want all the sordid details, but I wasn't raised to bury my head in the sand.

He cocks his head to the side a bit and narrows his eyes. "My marriage is none of your business, Levi."

"Do you really expect me to live in a fantasy with you, pretending that you don't have a wife and a passel of kids waiting for you back home? If that's the case, we don't need to be having any conversation at all." When he doesn't respond, I take a step back leaving my words to linger in the space between us.

I guess I shouldn't be shocked. Really, I mean, I shouldn't, but I at least expected something other than more silence from him when I mentioned the reality of the situation. And let's be honest, there isn't a situation to begin with, but him coming through here, into my world, and staking claims on me and making promises he can't fucking keep is starting pluck my last god damn nerve.

I nod and shrug my shoulders. "Typical."

Without sparing another glance in his direction, I give him my back and walk over to my closet, grabbing the first pair of black jeans I get my hands on and one of my favorite pearl snap shirts I'd stolen from my brother Addison. It was the same one I'd always worn when I went to shows, and because I'd started going to shows again just to be around horses in some capacity, it just felt right to pull it out. I was sometimes nostalgic like that. I might not ride anymore, but I missed competing—I missed my horses. I had bought land with them in mind for fuck's sake. No one knew that I did except for Thiago and now Cortland, which meant Alessio knows, and that didn't sit right with me.

As I emerge from my closet, clothes in hand, I see Cortland sitting in the emerald green velvet wingback chair tucked in the corner of my bedroom. Ignoring him, I stop in front of my dresser and toss my clothes onto the chaise next to it before stripping down completely. My shirt is barely over my head when I feel the weight of his gaze on my back. I take a deep, cleansing breath and shake off the nerves clawing their way up my throat, shutting down the crippling anxiety I haven't felt since the first time he'd stripped me bare.

I do my best to pretend he doesn't exist when I shove my shorts down my hips and they pool around my feet. A sharp intake of breath catches my attention, but I resist the urge to turn around. Opening the top drawer, I riffle through the mess until I find what I'm looking for.

It might've been confusing to Cortland to see what I have in my hand, but he doesn't comment.

There's a level of intimacy having someone watching you get dressed, differently than if you were undressing for or in front of them. It's such a mundane task, one you don't even really think about when doing it, but this was different. Having Cortland sit there in my bedroom, in my chair, watching me as I get ready is a sweet torture I wasn't prepared for.

Maybe it's because he is seeing me for the first time since I'd transitioned, or maybe it's because I am doing this knowing he was dying to touch me but can't, and now he was the one having to endure for me rather than the other way around.

Without thinking much of it, I bend over and slip each leg through the black thong. The tight fabric snaps against the skin of my hips once I finish adjusting the material, and I hear Cortland clear his throat, and I can't help smiling to myself.

A calloused hand curls around my hip, squeezing until it's just this side of painful. He pulls my hips into him until my ass meets his groin. We both groan when his cock splits my crease and he grinds into me, adding more pressure this time until I feel the roughness of his jeans scrap against my tender flesh like he's trying to brand himself on me.

"Don't ever walk away from me again, peach." He snarls, his teeth nipping at the nape of my neck.

7

CORTLAND

'Intoxicated' Warren Zeiders

A scrap of fabric is all it takes to get me on my feet. It perfectly bisected the two mouthwatering ass cheeks in front of me, making them look even rounder. The black straps nearly disappear into the ink scrawled across Levi's hips and flanks. I don't know what I was expecting to find beneath his clothes when he started pulling them off right in front of me, but this was so much more. I wanted to take my time looking at every single detail of the artwork blanketing his skin to unravel even a fraction of who he'd become, but that was for another time.

Like a magnet, I can't resist being pulled in his direction.

Before I even realize what I'm doing, I'm standing behind him, and it feels like déjà vu except this time I won't be fumbling and rushing in the dark where everyone can see Levi come apart at the seams for me.

My hand dwarfs his hip as I pull him against me until my pelvis meets his ass. An animalistic groan punches its way from my throat at the contact, and all I can do is ride out the pleasure and pain as Levi grinds into me. After watching him strip down to nothing, my cock is painfully hard. But getting even the smallest glimpse of his cunt made me feel like a starving man.

Even as I back off to find some relief, Levi chases the loss of contact like he can't get enough. My fingers intertwine with the strips of fabric resting on his hips, and I pull, watching my fingers and the skimpy material bite into his supple flesh. The contrast of his skin against mine is unlike anything I've experienced. I can't even begin to explain it.

Where mine is worn by necessity, his is worn by choice.

Levi could've chosen anything, but he still chose competing in some aspect of his life with the same level of risk and dedication while getting his hands ravaged by metal and gasoline.

It's no secret I've had my share of partners over the years, long before Levi and after him, yet he's always been the mold, the impossible standard, and he doesn't even know it.

"Vi," I manage between uneven breaths as I struggle to get my skyrocketing heart rate under control. "Fuck, what you do to me."

It doesn't make sense. No matter how badly I want to sink into him, I feel frozen. There's nothing holding me back in this moment other than the consequences. Too many variables rolling around my mind to think straight, and Levi grinding into me like his life depends on it isn't making it any easier to untangle the mess. A mess we're the nexus of.

His head rests on my shoulder, exposing his throat to me. Like a moth to a flame, I bury my nose in the delicate skin, inhaling until I can't pull in anymore of his delicious scent. My lungs burn while I attempt to hold as much of him inside me as I can, letting him brand me from the inside, before letting go. Not to purge my system of him, but so I can go back as many times he'll let me.

Not a day has gone by that I don't miss his banter or his sharp tongue, but most of all I miss the way he always smelled of peaches, mint, and horses. The smell had become so ingrained in his cells he couldn't get away from it—now the rich essence of baled hay, grain, and leather was replaced by gasoline and nicotine.

Levi lets out a startled yelp as my arms band around his torso, lifting him off the ground, and I drag him over to his bed. Without ceremony, I toss him onto the mattress still covered in sheets stained by cum and sweat. It would've been depraved and utterly emasculating to most men, but I don't give a shit. Levi won't be able to look at his bed and think of anyone other than me when I'm done with him—I'll make sure of it.

He doesn't bother with a façade of guilt or shame when he settles into the sheets. He just lets his thighs fall open, and I'm rendered speechless.

A glimpse wasn't enough. Miles of creamy flesh unblemished, uninterrupted like a quiet morning before the world wakes up and wreaks havoc. Closely trimmed, fine black hair dust the mound of soft flesh hidden between his thighs and I want nothing more than to bury my face in his crotch, suffocating on his scent.

His cunt drips with need as a tremor breaks out across his body while my gaze rakes over him. I study him, like I have so many times before, and it won't ever be enough. Nothing inside me ever felt satisfied, even when Levi gave me what I wanted. I still want more. Crave it. *Him.*

My mouth waters at the very sight of him, his hardened cock jutted from his slit, swollen and flushed. *So pretty.* He could easily ignore me, take matters into his own hands, but instead his hands remain fisted at his sides like the good boy I knew he could be. It's overwhelming—restraint and need at war within me.

"What are you waiting for, cowboy?" Levi taunts, his voice taking on a higher pitch as his frustration comes to the surface.

My pulse thrums, heart pounding. Control slips away from me, the edges of my vision blurring, narrowing as I stand between Levi's waiting thighs. He reaches for me, and I go willingly. His touch scorches my skin each time his nimble fingers brush against my abdomen while he pulls my shirt over my head.

It looks like he's swallowed his tongue when he glances in my direction, doing a double take after tossing my shirt aside.

Levi's eyes immediately fall to the brand on my left pec before stumbling over his words. "What the fuck?" He looks up at me in shock, mouth hanging open, waiting for some explanation. A tentative, unsure hand reaches out to trace the scarred tissue, his eyes turn blue from unshed tears.

"You never asked, baby." I knew what he meant, but I wasn't in the mood to get sidetracked, so I nudged his chin, closing his mouth before covering it with my own. I can taste desecration on his lips, and it has never been so sweet. I listen to his whimpering for a moment before swallowing them down until there is no protest left in him.

His tongue probes against my lips, and with no other warning he plunges his way into my mouth, reacquainting himself. My jaw clicks the further he pushes into my mouth, covering every inch he can reach as though he's trying to erase anyone who came before him. I wonder if he realizes he's doing it although it's unnecessary.

We may have done this before, but there is a different significance now that neither of us would be ready to acknowledge any time soon. *What ifs* plagued both of us, but I'd nurtured the level of mistrust Levi felt toward me. Even as I grip his waist and lift, shifting him further up the bed until my body covers his with ease, I know he would run again.

His lips brush my jaw, teeth grazing the skin. My cock twitches from the sudden pain and precum drips onto his thigh. Without thinking, I swipe up the precum and shove my forefinger into his mouth just to chase it with my own, to get even the slightest taste of me on his lips. He cranes into me and kisses me until the air in my lungs burns. Chest heaving, I slip my hand between his thighs, dipping the same finger inside of him before spreading his slick over his cock. I slot my forefinger and middle finger on either side and slowly stroke his cock until he mewls beneath me.

"Harder, fuck, Cortland," he demands in a breathy tone.

"Say please, boy," I purr, lips brushing over the shell of his ear, making him tremble against me.

Levi shakes his head and let out a cute, pathetic whine. I ignore him, lightening the pressure, only teasing the tip of his pretty little cock. He wrenches his eyes open, furious, and levels me with a glare.

"Say it."

He huffs indignantly. "Please." And rolls his fucking eyes.

I slap his cunt, making him squeal like a bitch and draw his legs closed. I shove his legs apart while he fights to keep them clamped together, caging him against the bed before doing it again. "Say it, Levi. Again."

A whimper escapes him, and emerald irises snap to mine, his eyes red and glassy.

"*Please.*" He pleads again and again until I kiss his sweaty temple, soothing him.

I palm his pussy, grinding the heel of my hand against his cock and sinking two fingers inside of him. I stretch him just enough, his cunt already sloppy and wet, before adding a third. I massage his inner walls until he quiets a moment. A tremor runs through his body, and he bows off the bed as I pull and press my fingers into the front wall of his hole. He keens, his teeth sinking into his lip. His cunt drips slick, but I want more. I grab the bottle of lube still sitting on his nightstand and pop the cap.

"Relax for me, peach." I say, my voice dripping in lust. I withdraw my fingers from inside him and drizzle lube onto them before sinking inside of him again. He whines at the intrusion but presses into me. I add a fourth finger and kiss his neck, encouraging him.

"I can't. I can't, Cortland. Please." He rambles, but I don't let up. I watch as his breathing hitches, and he rocks his body slightly, but he doesn't tell me stop.

Levi gives himself over to the pleasure and pain as my knuckles slip inside of him.

"So gorgeous." The words fall from my lips without permission as I stare down at our connection, entranced by what's in front of me. His hole was clinging to nearly all of my hand, the inflamed tissue stretched, glistening and pulsing around me and trying to suck me deeper, and I couldn't tear my eyes away even if I tried.

I dip down and suck his neglected cock between my lips, pulling it between my teeth. His hands find their way into my hair and fist the strands, pulling until my scalp burns as I sink my tongue beneath his cock, giving him one last nip of my teeth, and it earns me a shrill scream that warms my chest.

He squirms against me as I work my tongue inside him alongside my fingers, soothing the inflamed, reddened tissue. His scream mellows into a staccato of moans as he floods my mouth and drenches my chin. I pull my fingers from his hole, watching it clench around nothing while he writhes beneath me. Not even bothering to wipe my face, I lean down and slant my lips over his, giving him a taste of himself, and he groans.

Levi's tongue finds my chin, his teeth nipping me until I move how he wants me, and he cleans my face. Broad, firm strokes of his tongue along my jaw, lips, and chin, heat settling in my groin and forcing my attention back to my cock, throbbing and heavy between my legs.

He swallows thickly around a moan he tries to stifle, but I rip it from his throat, his cock trapped between the knuckles of my middle and forefinger, and he screams so beautifully for me. His abdomen concaves, and he dips his hips further into the mattress, trying to run from me, but I can't have that.

My cock rubbed against the back of his thigh, and I nipped his bottom lip, "You can take it for me, Levi."

A small mewl, almost a whimper, drips from his lips, and his eyes turn glassy and unfocused, but his body relaxes, legs falling open beneath me, and I lick into his mouth, tasting his cries.

His taste on my tongue is like a kill switch, emptying my mind until all I see is him—until all I feel is his heart beating for me.

I glance down between us, his cunt weeping and puffy from the abuse, and his cock throbbing so hard I can see it pulsing, almost quivering. I use his slick that dripped between his ass cheeks to force my thumb into his asshole. My fingers stretch him to the point of pain, but as I pull on his rim, his legs start to shake uncontrollably. His body seizes, and I move between his legs, shouldering them apart and latch onto his pussy until his piss fills my mouth. An almost earthy yet musky essence coats my tongue as I drink everything he has to offer, and I can't get enough.

He was the only one I'd ever tasted like this, even when I'd been tempted by a partner in the past and no matter how much they begged, I'd only indulge it with Levi.

It's bittersweet, trying to reconcile with myself that I made the right choice eight years ago to let him go just to have him like this beneath me, knowing I could be leaving him wide open to those who would rather see him six feet under than breathing by my side as the person he was always meant to be—my heart almost couldn't handle it. There isn't much that could make me question my choices, but Levi would every single time. Too many *what ifs* screamed in my mind, and if I let them get too loud, too painful, I'd lose everything, including him. Many times, I'd wanted to cut and run, leave everything behind to bring Levi home, but the risks were too high, and he deserved to live—with or without me. But now that I had him again, I refused to entertain what my life would be like without him. It was a constant war within my mind, and eventually it was going to play out in front of me. It was just a matter of time.

But for now, my hands would stay glued to him if my lips weren't already. Levi lets out a sigh of relief and starts to draw his legs closed as my fingers leave his abused holes, his eyes drifting to mine for a moment before sinking closed. He looks so peaceful like this, almost like a sleeping cat you ought not mess with, but I'm not done.

My hand comes down on his inner thigh, striking the soft flesh hard enough to leave a mark but also to bring his focus back to me. He yelps, pathetically, and a laugh rumbles in my chest. His hand comes up abruptly, and I lean out of his reach before it connects with my cheek.

"Oh, peach. You can do better than that." I say as I snatch his wrist firmly, the tendons and bones rolling beneath his flesh. His emerald irises flare, and he shoots up from the bed nearly knocking me off balance, his chest heaving.

Before he has a chance to fix his mouth to say something bratty, I let go of his wrist in favor of his throat and squeeze, my thumb digging into his carotid. He snarls, his lip curling, and I kiss him anyway. It's a mess of teeth and saliva, but he becomes pliant under my hands like an obedient little thing. He goes willingly when I nudge him to turn over onto his front, and I can't stop myself from kneading the soft expanse of his thighs, holding him in place for a moment. His ass hikes up in the air, hips swaying while he looks over his shoulder, eyes burning with lust.

Unable to resist the sight in front of me, I bury my face in his pussy, nuzzling his saliva, piss-stained flesh, and inhale. He starts to squirm, tilting his hips to get away from me, but I hold him there until I've had my fill of him. I slowly lick around his cock before dipping my tongue inside him again, his tissue swollen and tender from the rough treatment I'd already given, and he tries to pull away. I give him a light slap on the back of his thigh, and he settles against me, giving me access to him without complaint.

He lurches forward in surprise as my tongue circles his deprived asshole but chases the sensation when I go to pull away, and I laugh into his damp skin, making him groan from the unexpected sensation. His rim starts to give under the pressure of my tongue, and I slide my tongue inside him—unable to stop myself, I groan along with him.

His hips start to rock against me when I start stroking his cock in time with my tongue fucking into his ass, and he's right where I want him before I pull away completely, leaving him gasping at the sudden loss.

"Don't get too comfortable. I'm not done with you yet, boy." His body goes stock still, rigid beneath me before I even follow through with delivering another slap on his already bruised ass cheek.

I loosen my hold on him and let him fall into a heap. He curls in on himself and averts his gaze. This isn't a drop like any I'd experienced before; this was something else entirely, and I don't know if Levi was even conscious of what was happening now. I wait for a moment, waiting for him to say something or to even look my way, but he clams up even further. His body trembles like he caught a chill, and his breathing becomes thready, much too thin, even with his chest beginning to heave like he's trying to pull in any amount of air he possibly can.

Rather than give him space, I curl myself around him, leg thrown over his hip and my arms pulling his body into me. I whisper for him to calm his breathing, to count any random objects in our vicinity until his breathing evens out and he turns in my arms, burrowing into my chest. With the lightest touch possible, I stroke his side, hoping the repetitive movement can somehow ground him. He looks up at me for a moment, his pupils dilated with welled tears lining his lash line and his scleras nearly beat red from the blood vessels agitated from stress. It doesn't last longer than a minute before he nuzzles into me, trying to hide from the world.

I don't know how long we stay like this, but if he needs it, I'll give it to him. I was aware of how his father treated him before he ever came out, but he never told me anything about it...I just saw the bruises that he tried to place off as riding accidents and other bullshit excuses that never added up. He was a flawless rider, and the bruises almost always looked like they were handprints seared into his skin. Sometimes there were welts from the ring his father always wore.

Levi bristles against me, my hand stilling along his ribcage, and a whine breaks free from him when I start to pull away. He instantly wraps himself around my body to prevent me from moving, and I let him.

When lips wrap around my nipple, my body immediately jerks, and I look down to find Levi with his eyes closed and his mouth firmly suctioned to my chest, sucking and pulling until I groan. Before I question it, I support his head right below his occipital bone, holding him closer. I ignore my stiff length, cursing myself for getting hard while he's using my body to seek comfort. My dick is beyond angry at this point, having ignored it for God knows how long now, but whatever is going on in Levi's head, whatever made him clam up, would always be more important. My eyes sink closed while I allow him to soothe himself, hard-on be damned.

Tentative licks rouse me again, and the little fuck looks up at me, arousal flaring in his eyes. He knows exactly what he's doing and doesn't even bother to look guilty.

"Keep fuckin' with me, Levi, and you won't like where you end up by the time I'm done," I threaten, though it sounds weak to my ears as a groan creeps up my throat, and my hips rock into him.

Levi arches a single black brow then sinks his teeth into the oversensitive bud, earning a moan from me. He pops off with a loud smack and licks his lips slowly like a cat who got the canary. Cold hands wrap around my cock and give a firm tug, my body crashing into his for a moment. He strokes my cock until precum stains his abdomen.

A grin splits his handsome face as he swipes up every drop onto his fingers. I expect him to lick his fingers clean, but what he does instead would drive even the sanest man to his knees.

I watch his precum drenched fingers dip inside his pussy, mingling with his slick before he brings them back to his swollen cock. He strokes my cock in time with his own. His chest heaves as he sucks in a deep breath, his abdomen concaving and hips sinking further into the mattress.

"What was that, cowboy?" He exhales, his cadence shuddering as his body quakes. His hand tightens almost painfully around my cock, nearly pulling my orgasm to the surface. He abruptly lets go and snakes his hand to my balls, giving them a rough tug. A wicked smirk plays on his swollen lips, and his knee connects with my ribs, shoving me off him until I end up on my back beneath him. As my back hits the mattress, I frown at him, lips parting in confusion for a moment.

Levi straddles my waist, and he looks down at me,

triumphant. He looks like a damn angel. With no other warning, he pushes my cock inside his dripping cunt. He opens up around me, inviting me in so easily, hot and wet. I plant my feet on the mattress, and I snap my hips up each time he starts his descent. He finds a rhythm, rising and falling on my cock, intent on breaking me. My teeth set under the pressure mounting inside me while I stave off my impending orgasm that's been creeping its way up since he grabbed me by the balls.

"You're so quiet, baby. What happened, hmm? Cat got your tongue?" He teases, all while his voice is shattering on each syllable.

He sinks down on me, slowly, resting a hand on my chest for support and uses it to his advantage. His cock grinds into my pubic bone, allowing him to deepen his pleasure without asking for more from me. I watch as the angel I thought he looked like for a moment turns demonic, his pupils swallowing emerald, blackening his eyes, and the tendons in his neck sharpening.

My hands find their way onto his hips, gripping the supple flesh and pulling his body further into mine, his lips landing on mine. I swallow his moan as his free hand encases my throat, and he squeezes, my pulse jumping in anticipation. He sits back up, body quivering, and undulates his hips, pulling me in further. His velvet walls cling to my cock, dragging against the swollen tissue, and he slaps my chest, biting his lip to contain the pitiful noises he can't seem to get a handle on.

"What's wrong, peach? I thought you could handle it."

His movements come to an abrupt stop, and he clenches around me, effectively shutting me up, only hurtling me closer to my own orgasm. He seems to sniff it out as my hips stutter, and he plants his left hand on my thigh, nails digging into the muscle just enough to distract me. His other hand massages my balls, almost petting them, before he tugs them sharply—he's good at ruining orgasms it seems, the fucker.

I watch my length disappear inside of him, over and over. It's hypnotizing to witness, and I don't want him to stop. His body consumes mine so readily, like it was made for me.

He doesn't bother with finesse. It's messy and disjointed as he chases another orgasm, and my body is just here to facilitate it. He hasn't looked at me once, his head thrown back, exposing the vulnerable expanse of his throat to me as more needy moans and whimpers float around us.

I keep my hand at the small of his back, and with the smallest amount of pressure, I tilt his pelvis into mine, forcing his neglected cock to absorb each slap completely each time I drive my hips into his. His hand tightens around my throat, and his nails bite into my skin as his pussy clamps onto my cock, pulsing around me while he comes, drenching my cock and pelvis.

Levi's head hangs between his shoulders, his eyes glazed over, and his ass rocks into me despite the duality of pleasure and pain igniting in his eyes. The walls of his pussy tighten around me, spasming and pulling me deeper. I grip his hips, holding him in place as I snap my hips up once more, making him take all of me. A familiar tingling at the base of my spine is the only warning I have before I spill inside of him, groaning as my cum paints his walls. His pussy slackens, releasing its hold on me, but I don't pull out. I stay inside him, not wanting to lose the connection.

He collapses in a heap on top of me, his damp breaths tickling my chest while he pants, unable to get his breathing under control as he comes down from the high. I rub his side, and because my control is shot at this point, I kiss his head, gathering him in my arms and turn over.

As his breathing evens out, I look down at him, memorizing every piece of him while he's softened in my arms. It shocks me for a moment, him trusting me enough to allow me to see him in such a vulnerable state, but I'll take it.

His warmth surrounds me, sleep sneaking up on me, pulling me into its depths until I surrender to it.

I JERK IN MY SLEEP, a buzzing vibrating through my sternum, needles pricking my chest repeatedly. Awareness claws at my mind, the sensation of being watched overwhelms my senses, but sleep pulls me back under as my body settles into the warmth of my bed.

Just a few more minutes. I need just a little bit longer before waking up to the nightmares around me.

A weight settles in my stomach like a ton of bricks, making breathing nearly impossible, heat flaring across my skin as needles dig into my chest again before releasing, only to sink deeper a third time.

My eyes snap open, light blinding me almost immediately before my eyes have time to adjust. The room is bathed in shadows and pre-dawn light where the curtains have been drawn by someone. Oxblood walls surrounded me, adorned with ornate frames and oddities on every manageable surface.

The realization hits me a second too late—I'm not in my hotel room; I never made it back to Atlanta last night. I was in Levi's bed, basking in the comfort of his scent.

Amber eyes sear into me atop my chest, soft fur brushing against my skin, tickling my stomach. Again, claws dig into my skin, ripping me open wider than they had before. I stay perfectly still, my breathing slowing until the creature staring into my soul stops moving, and I wait for him to move first.

A dark chuckle meets my ears from somewhere in the

room, but I don't see Levi, at least not immediately. I look in the mirror hanging above the chest of drawers and see him leaning against the doorframe at the threshold of the en suite.

"Are you fucking scared of cats, Thierry? Seriously?" He jokes, his laugh grating my nerves.

"No, I'm not scared of them. I just don't mess with them if I don't have to." I grumble like an errant child that had been caught doing something they ought not be.

He steps further into the room, his long legs eating up the distance until his thigh brushes the edge of the mattress, and he has the nerve to pet the creature still perched on my chest, completely unbothered by the predicament I'm in.

Levi coos at the devious bastard while he slowly blinks at me. His purring radiates through my bones as Levi runs his fingers through his dense fur. They're so much alike when they receive affection, chasing it as soon as they get the barest amount. I watch each time Levi starts to pull his hand away from the greedy little thing, but he immediately sought out Levi's hand, not to be deterred.

"You're staring, cowboy. Didn't your momma tell you that was rude?" Levi says, his voice filled with humor. He lifts his gaze from the feline and meets mine head on, and his eyes soften for a moment before his walls erect back into place.

"Probably. Knowing her, she always had rules I never followed, so why start now?" He slaps my thigh playfully with the back of his hand and rolls his eyes, fighting the smile pulling at the corners of his decadent lips.

"Spade will keep you occupied, but do get out of my bed. I have things to do, none of which involve you." With that, he leaves me and walks back to the bathroom.

Spade–that's the little shit's name–peers down at me before stretching his long body, clawing my chest yet again and making me gasp at the stinging pain. His long tail nearly whips me in the face when he jumps down, slinking off to who knows where.

I force my old bones to move and grab the first pair of sweatpants I find in his drawers, pulling them on quickly and following him into the bathroom. He doesn't acknowledge my presence while he undresses and steps under the boiling water, steam wafting its way through the spacious bathroom. I watch as he goes through each step of what I assume to be his routine in the shower and wait for him to turn back around.

"You're staring again. It's unseemly at this point. You should be embarrassed." He purrs, taunting me. It doesn't stop him from glancing over his shoulder, his hand snaking its way between his thighs, cleaning himself while my eyes feast on every bit of naked flesh in front of me.

I was going to get him dirty again, but he was already in the shower, and I'm not complaining, especially when I get to watch the water slide over his flesh, washing away the suds that coat his body. What started as a mundane task devolved quickly, sexual tension saturating the air between us. He isn't going to invite me in, but he knows he has me by the balls.

"Levi, get on your knees," I say, my voice raspier than normal, even to my own ears.

He cocks his head to the side and arches a brow in my direction. "Can't seem to control yourself, huh?" It wasn't a question. We both knew it was a fact.

I shove my borrowed sweatpants down my hips just enough to get his attention and start stroking my cock to motivate him. I jut out my chin to remind him of exactly what I want and wait.

The hunger in his eyes is undeniable as he watches me fist my length, and I suppress a groan from working its way up my throat the moment he starts watching me.

What could I say? I'm a sucker for this man's eyes to be on me at all times.

When he finally obeys, he takes his fucking time, torturing me as he eases down onto his knees. He's not modest, but he keeps his knees together and simply grins. Soap is still lathered over his skin, dripping down between his thighs. It's all I can do not to walk over to him and kick them apart so I can see every part of him on display for me.

Fuck it.

"You actin' all shy ain't gonna work with me, boy," I murmur as I continue working over my cock without looking away from him for even a second as I make my way over to the shower. His grin grows wider somehow—completely maniacal and unhinged, just the way I like him.

For a moment, I stay rooted in place, leaning against the cool tile of the shower wall admiring everything he is. I'd already seen every part of him, from head to toe, but it's like I'm seeing him for the first time again. He couldn't be more perfect. The scar running down the left side of his face from a trail accident, the slight bump at the bridge of his nose from the time he'd got bucked from the same horse in his family's arena, and somehow each piercing and tattoo flowed effortlessly down to the ones covering his boney feet. Even the scars he was so afraid for me to see–whether he would admit to it or not, I knew he was terrified. Every inch of him trembling as he stripped down in front of me, though he has nothing to be ashamed of, least of all with me. And he should know by now I would remind him with words, with touch, everyday if I thought it would soothe his anxiety.

Faint scars etch into the skin of his chest beneath his pectorals—they're subtle, hardly even there, but I know they mean more than that to him. They're not just haphazard. It wasn't a decision he made irrationally. He made it so he was able to breathe, able to look at himself in the mirror and know who he was looking at without any doubt in his mind that the person looking back at him is worth every loss, every sacrifice, he made to live.

He was as breathtaking then as he is now but having him on his knees for me when he's whole and so sure of himself is more than I ever thought I would be capable of having when I finally laid eyes on him again.

Without a word, I kick open his legs and step between them, making him lose some of his balance, and he immediately recenters himself to stay upright. His knees skid across the shower tile, squelching along the slick surface, but his cock is swollen and throbbing anyway. I knew he loved humiliation, but I'd been careful yesterday not to send him running. Now, he's getting what he craves, and I have no intention of holding back.

My hand shoots out to grab his jaw, keeping his eyes on me. "Never hide what's mine from me again, peach. I want unfettered access at any time, and I intend to keep it that way with or without your say," I promise, just shy of threatening him. The ligaments of his jaw tense beneath my hold, but I don't ease up, not even a bit.

He whimpers, pitifully, as he strains against my legs still keeping his knees apart, preventing him from relief. His lip trembles while he looks up at me.

He looks so adorable when he's frustrated. Like an enraged kitten, so small but ready to spit nails.

"Is that all you got? I thought you'd at least try a little harder than that to get what you want, but that was pathetic, peach. I expected more from you." I sigh, barely containing the laugh threatening to escape. I want him to fight. I want him desperate enough that he'll shatter into a million pieces when I finally give him just an ounce of reprieve.

Levi holds himself together a bit longer before making another weak attempt to force me to give in to him. He tightens his thighs once more, and while it doesn't get him anywhere near where he wants to be, it exhausts him enough to make him just a bit more pliant. The grind of his muscle and bone against mine grounds me enough to drag this out a while longer than either of us wants.

A symphony of his heavy panting and whimpering echo off the marble tile while he struggles against me, and I can't resist fisting my cock, stroking it over his face until he starts to thrash uncontrollably. My little peach tries to get closer. A desperate moan meets my ears when I lean out of his reach, and a grin tugs at my lips. His glassy half-lidded gaze lands on me, green eyes turning blue like an enraged tidal wave, and his brows furrow like he might have something to say just to be spiteful.

There's a sweetness to his fight that I've never been able to get from anyone else, and it ignites something within me that I can't quite place. Even though I've been in this exact position with many other men, even women, something about it being Levi makes everything fall into place like it was always meant to.

"Now, I want you to listen to me very carefully, yeah?" Without hesitation, Levi nods, keeping his emerald gaze on me. "Keep your knees apart, put your hands behind your back and tilt your head back for me. Don't move from where you're kneeling. And always, keep your eyes on me, peach."

I take a step back and study each movement, committing them to memory as he does as he's told. He knows what's coming. His body is already vibrating from anticipation, and I'd be lying if I said I didn't have some level of doubt going into this.

I saw the way he reacted to Nyx, and it made me curious. Hell, I watched him practically huffing the scent of me from Nyx's sweaty, piss stained skin while he was holding him up. I felt bad for the kid, but Alessio wasn't planning on letting him go before each of us had a turn on him that night. By the time I'd gotten my hands on him, I'd wanted to give him a break, but I knew better, and deep down I didn't care enough to walk out. Nyx was already high out of his mind by then after snorting multiple lines of cocaine Alessio had given him, but he was too agreeable, too compliant, for it to have ended with just the cocaine. White residue dusted his nostrils as he'd been looking up at me while he'd drank every bit of what I'd given him like it was the first liquid to touch his lips in days. Whether Alessio slipped him something else at any point before he arrived, I don't know. I didn't fucking ask either. The impression I had was Nyx had consented, and it wasn't my place to question Alessio. When Jameson showed up, not a single person was surprised by the state of Nyx. Levi hadn't been either.

Their nonreaction spoke volumes.

I never claimed to be a good man, and I wasn't, but I never thought I'd question my own morals in favor of guaranteeing the safety of those I'd loved. Alessio had me by the balls, and we both know it. While Levi didn't ask me about that night, I wonder what went through his head, if he knew what I'd done to keep him and my family safe. And if he did, would he still look at me like I was worth something?

As I look down at him, in this very moment, I know I would sacrifice any piece of me if it meant he was still breathing, with or without me. I would do it every single time.

A slight blush creeps up Levi's neck under the weight of my gaze, but he doesn't say anything—he just waits. The level of trust he seems to still have in me feels too good to be true. I keep waiting for him to wake up and realize I couldn't be a worse choice for him, that he deserves better than me, but I'm too damn selfish to even put the idea in his head.

I don't even bother with a warning. Levi gasps as my piss

hits his collarbone and his pupils dilate. I watch in rapt fascination as it trickles down his chest, meeting the beads of water from the shower, but it doesn't satiate the burning need to mark him the way I so desperately need.

I want to curse the water for washing away any remnants of my scent on him. I want every inch of him to smell of me, leaving no one to question who he belongs to.

He doesn't flinch as urine hits his cheekbones and drips down his chin—he chases it. His pink tongue tentatively peeks out of his mouth before he tries to swipe up what remains and like he already knows what I want, he adjusts his posture without much movement and keeps his mouth open for me. I rest my forearm on the tile above his head and shift my hips enough to fill his mouth with my cock. He doesn't suck, just holds my cock in his mouth while I flood his waiting mouth. The convulsion as his throat works to swallow every drop of piss I give him forces him to suck, and my fist slaps against the wet tile as my cock hardens in the warm depths of his lush mouth.

Levi moans and the vibration along my shaft pulls a groan from me. It's almost painful how hard he makes me every damn time. He doesn't even have to try. It's just Levi.

"Don't waste it, peach. Every drop," I say, my voice sounding foreign to my own ears. I palm the back of his head, winding the messy black curls between my fingers and jerking him closer, my cock nearly bruising the back of his throat before pulling back as he swallows around me.

My hips drive forward until I meet resistance, and I wait a moment for his throat to relax enough to accommodate my cock. With the last spurt of piss leaving my bladder to settle in his throat, I lean down to lick into his mouth, swirling my tongue around his and licking every inch of him I can reach. The musky, almost malted essence of urine remaining on his tongue overwhelms my senses. His teeth shutter, grazing the side of my tongue as I lick across his gums before sucking his lower lip into my mouth.

His chest heaves as he whimpers into my mouth, desperation bleeding into his thready cadence, "Cortland, please."

I hum under my breath as I break away from him and give him one lasting stroke of my tongue up his chin, leaving him with a kiss on his forehead. "Mine."

No longer holding him steady, he drops to the floor, gasping once more. I watch as he curls in on himself, thighs shaking from the effort of holding himself together for me, his knees reddened by the individual honey-combed tiles digging into his flesh, leaving the pattern branded on him. A sharp whine leaves his swollen lips. It's almost shrill, deafening, but mellows after a moment.

I sink to my knees in front of him and pull his body into mine. His legs wrap around my waist while my hands knead the soft expanse of skin just above his hips bones, pulling him closer until there is no discernible way of telling us apart. We devolve into silence, observing one another.

In our reprieve, we linger. He doesn't push for more even though I see it so clearly in his eyes—he's aching.

"Please," he sighs against my lips once more, his eyes red rimmed and glassy. "I need it."

"Need what, hmm? Tell me, Levi. Use your words." I muse, wanting his words. I need to hear it in his voice.

"Your mouth, cowboy." His voice shatters on my name, his teeth chattering as he tries to get closer.

I place a hand on his chest, pushing against his sternum until his shoulders meet the tiled floor, carefully lifting his hips as his legs unwind from my waist. His eyes sink closed on a moan as I close my mouth over his pussy. I flatten my tongue beneath his swollen cock, gathering salty fluid and swallowing him down. His nails dig into my thigh, biting into the muscle as he shakes.

"Look at me or I'll stop." I threaten, his eyes snapping open at my roughened cadence.

Levi covers his mouth as he struggles to keep his on me, trying to dampen the sounds shattering the silence around us. I push my tongue inside him and watch as he comes apart in my arms. His lashes flutter along his tear-stained cheeks, teeth sinking into his bottom lip and tearing at the soft tissue until a bead of blood came to the surface. His cock pulses against my tongue, throbbing with need.

My mind goes quiet as I suck him into my mouth, listening to his whimpering turn guttural when I slide two fingers deep inside him and press against the front wall of his cunt.

I didn't wait for him to adjust before grinding my knuckles into the soft tissue protecting his urethra until his screams took over and his legs began to shake, flooding my mouth for what felt like the hundredth time, and it still wouldn't be enough. He drenched my chin while I lapped up every bit of what I wrung out of him. His cries grew weaker, hiccupping on a sob while I soothed the inflamed tissues. *Beautiful.*

I remove my fingers from his reddened hole and spread his puffy, swollen lips until his cock juts forward. I wrap my lips around his cock, sucking hard, teeth grazing the sensitized nerves until he comes. He whimpers and thrashes against me weakly. *Pitiful.* He pushes back, thighs squeezing my head while he fights the excruciating pleasure. As he comes down from the adrenaline, panic sets in, but I latch on and wait for his thighs to fall open once more. As they relax, I lessen the suction I had on him and lick around his cock until he sighs into me.

A phone ringing shatters the silence that's fallen over us,

bursting the bubble around us. I ignore it until it stops ringing, hoping Levi will ignore it as well. An annoyed sigh leaves him, his knee glancing off my cheek while he pushes me away from him and struggles to stand. I try to help him get on his feet, but I throw my hands up in the air when he swats them away. And the phone starts ringing again.

"It's yours, Cortland. Get out of the shower." He bites out, each word like a knife to the chest as he walks away from me.

The reality of our situation starts setting in faster than I want it to, but there is nothing I could do to stop it. Levi knew the score, and so did I. I just didn't want to settle up.

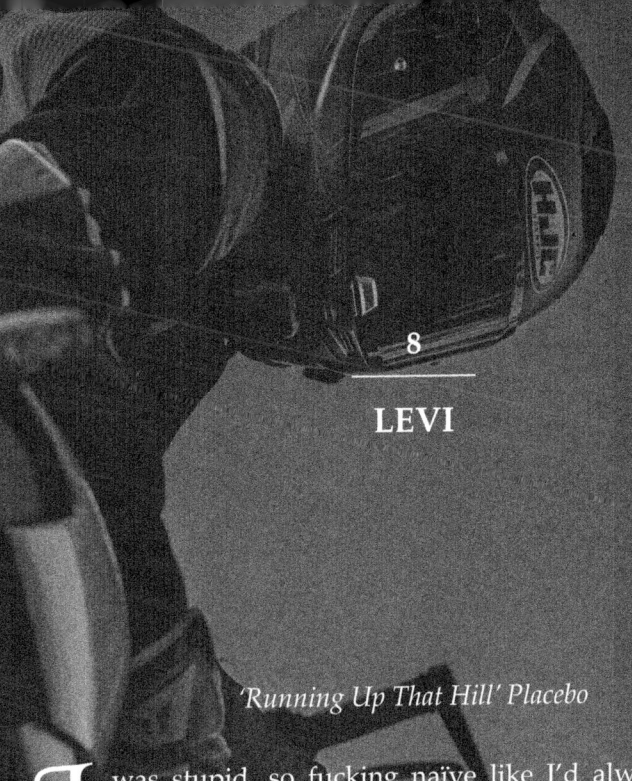

8

LEVI

'Running Up That Hill' Placebo

I was stupid, so fucking naïve like I'd always been. It wasn't as if I didn't understand the severity or believed there was a shot in hell for this to work. He's married.

I'd slept with a married man and now his wife's name is popping up on his phone repeatedly.

"Levi, it's not what you think." Words that had been said to so many men while the man they were fucking had a wife and family at home, waiting for them to come back to them.

I ignore Cortland, disappearing into my closet and throwing on any clothes I can get my hands on before storming out of my bedroom. My heart pounds, stomach in my throat while he calls out for me to come back, to hear him out, but I can't hear his voice over the static buzzing in my head.

He follows me through the house, grabbing my arm to stop me, only for me to shake him off. I swipe my bike keys on my way out the door, tears welling in my eyes.

I was so fucking stupid.

Without giving him another thought, I throw my leg over the body of my bike, the seat soothing my nerves, and my breathing slows. The sky opens up as I turn over the ignition, the cold start drowns his booming voice that echoes around me, closing in on me.

I drop my bike into gear, letting out the clutch and cranking the throttle. As I look in my side mirror, I can see him yelling for me, phone to his ear. I turned back for a moment, watching as he ripped open the driver's side door of his truck. I exhale, turning back around and pulling onto the stretch of road in front of my house, dropping another gear and gunning it, putting as much distance between us as I can manage before he comes after me.

Rain pelts my skin, ripping at my exposed forearms and chest. Wind whips through my soaked shirt, chilling me to the bone, but I don't care. My chest heaves as I take the fresh air into my lungs, my nose filling with carbon and the smell of gasoline. Green flashes around me, the trees and fields blurring into one while I take each breath, hoping to purge myself of him one last time, knowing damn well it would never be possible.

Each twist and turn through the backroads felt like a knife twisting deeper while I bled out for him. It was always me that ended up fucked, always ended up with the shit cards and as much as I run, it never goes away.

I don't know what I thought was going to happen this time, letting him back in and believing him, believing for a second that I was allowed to have what I wanted when it would never work out that way. Loving him had almost cost me my life before, and it still taxed me every day. Cortland had been given everything he wanted, but he wanted more, too much more.

He was messing with my head. Every touch, every look,

every hushed promise he thought I didn't hear, all of it flashed through my mind as I took each tight turn through winding roads I typically avoided.

The headlights of a truck flash in my side mirror, catching me off guard for a moment. Fucking asshole. I shake my head, returning my eyes to the road, but I'm a second too late —it was a rookie mistake.

Distraction allows my nerves to fray and accidental fixation on what was in front of me takes over too quickly. There is no place for anxiety when you could be seconds away from death. A single miscalculation, a moment of doubt would only result in leaving in a body bag. Hesitation was a silent killer; it bred a lack of control. I knew it better than anyone, it had left my skin black and blue, splitting under the weight of hands meant to keep me safe, meant to nurture.

I don't panic when I feel my bike start to slide out from under me like I would have expected. I allow it to happen, giving myself over to whatever comes next. As my skin meets the slick pavement, fire scorches every inch of my body. The ligaments and bones of my wrist scream in agony while I try to catch myself. My skull cracks against the pavement, fracturing my vision into stars, but a sense of calm washes over me. It's strange. Any time I'd imagined this moment, I had been terrified. Friends had gone down in front of me, and it was paralyzing. But I feel free. There is a serenity in it that I have never experienced before. My eyes sink closed, warmth greeting me, and I let go.

I should have waited. If I had just waited, if I had let him speak for just a moment, I wouldn't be here.

I am in and out of consciousness as someone pulls over on the shoulder, gravel crunching under their tires. Their door slams, making my head scream, and they slowly round the front of their vehicle.

"Yes, it just happened. She went down on one of the

turns," they say, their voice flat, almost clinical. I don't try to open my eyes as they crouch down in front of my body. Their hands are all over me, cataloguing, mapping out my injuries and relaying them to someone.

"No need. Her injuries will likely take care of it for us," they muse, delight tinging their voice for a moment before continuing, "No one will find her in time. It's done." A click brings me back to consciousness, but I relax under their skillful hands.

"You made this messier than it ever needed to be, Aubrey. Why couldn't you just let us do this humanely, hmm? You always had to make life more difficult, didn't you?" A new voice reverberates through my mind, penetrating the soft tissue. The familiarity of it sends ice through my veins.

A set of hands rips open the button of my jeans and yanks them down, the sound of the material splitting brought tears to my eyes. They bullied their way between my legs, shoving them apart as I tried to pull away, but their grip forced my body to stop fighting. Gravel digs into the back of my thighs and ass as they manipulate my body the way they want until I give up.

An acidic stench assaults my senses, their breath wafting over my face as they speak, "You always were a pretty thing, show pony."

The sound of metal teeth unzipping and the unbuckling of belts set my teeth on edge while I force myself to endure the calloused hands searing into my flesh like a branding iron. My jaw unhinges on a silent scream as my mind fractures, pain lancing through my core. Sudden weight crushes my larynx, forcing my eyes open at the shock of pain, but blackness welcomes me like an old friend.

"Tell me something, Bree. Do you think Cortland would want what's left of you when we're through with you?" One asked, ripping through soft tissue and setting me on fire. The more I struggle against the hands that held me down, sinister laughter echoes through the still air. "It's a pity you'll never find out."

The End...for now ;)

AFTERWORD

I know, I know. A cliffhanger sucks, but you made it.

Levi and Cortland's story became unbelievably more important to me the more time I spent with them for many reasons. The main one being giving a voice to not only other trans people close to me and myself, but for the one still afraid to live in their truth when they shouldn't have to be.

Levi is a very unique character. He has many, many layers, most of which I am still learning myself, but he is authentically and unapologetically himself. Though it took years for him to get there, he did it. And even if he is himself, he still has moments of doubt like we all do.

And Cortland, god that man. He is a pain in the ass, but he is who he is. He's very similar to Levi in that sense, that what you see is what you get. But he is undoubtedly Levi's biggest champion and protector, no matter how he chooses to do so.

These two have taken over my life for the past year or so and they are not going anywhere any time soon. We still have book two to get through, and I wish I could say it's going to get easier, but it wouldn't be me if I made it easy.

Afterword

Book 2 is set to come out before the end of this year and I will keep you guys updated throughout the process on all of my socials.

ACKNOWLEDGMENTS

I'm already uncomfortable trying to write this so just bear with me.

Marie, you have been in my life for what feels like an eternity and it still will never be enough. There are no amount of words that could ever encapsulate the gratitude and love I have for you. You have held it down for me through every stage of life, but also this book. You kept me sane through everything that I didn't understand how to do, and kept my head on as straight as it can be, which isn't saying much. Thank you for being you. Thank you for loving me the way you do. This book, these boys wouldn't be here without you. I love you. Go listen to the Grey for me.

My beta readers. You guys held my hand so many times through the many changes, through the frustration, the crash outs and you still stuck it out for me. I couldn't have done this without you.

And my readers, thank you. Thank you for trusting me to deliver this story, no matter how long it took me to get here. Many of you have seen me through major changes as well and I can't express how grateful I am to still have you.

Shoutout to the DumDums for keeping my ass from smoking like a freight train. And my pups, Zodiac and Mia, were flies on the wall for everything and even if they were judging me, they still love me anyway. I wouldn't be here without them.

ABOUT THE AUTHOR

Alex Kohl is an author who loves spending time with their pups, Mia and Zodiac, and usually has a book in their hand. They can be found attending concerts of their favorite bands who are probably featured in the playlists curated for each of their books. Alex draws inspiration for their characters and stories from anything they're obsessing over at any moment; whether that's a song, a quote or the need for something missing and turning it into something beautifully tragic and sometimes heart wrenching.

Printed in Dunstable, United Kingdom